# MULVANEY
# STORIES

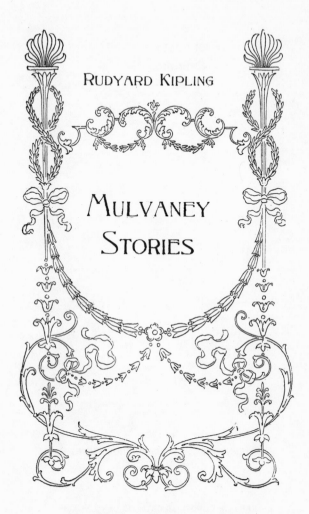

RUDYARD KIPLING

MULVANEY
STORIES

*Short Story Index Reprint Series*

BOOKS FOR LIBRARIES PRESS
FREEPORT, NEW YORK

First Published 1897
Reprinted 1971

INTERNATIONAL STANDARD BOOK NUMBER:
0-8369-4045-8


LIBRARY OF CONGRESS CATALOG CARD NUMBER:
70-178444


PRINTED IN THE UNITED STATES OF AMERICA
BY
NEW WORLD BOOK MANUFACTURING CO., INC.
HALLANDALE, FLORIDA 33009

# CONTENTS

( iii )

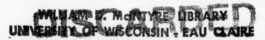

# THE THREE MUSKETEERS.

An' when the war began, we chased the bold Afghan,
An' we made the bloomin' Ghazi for to flee, boys O !
An' we marched into *Kabul*, and we tuk the Balar
    'Issar,
An' we taught 'em to respec' the British Soldier.
                      *Barrack Room Ballad.*

MULVANEY, Ortheris and Learoyd are privates in B Company of a line regiment, and personal friends of mine. Collectively, I think, but am not certain, they are the worst men in the regiment so far as genial blackguardism goes.

They told me this story, the other day, in the Umballa refreshment-room while we were waiting for an up-train. I supplied the beer. The tale was cheap at a gallon and a half.

Of course you know Lord Benira Trig. He is a duke, or an earl, or something unofficial; also a peer; also a globe-trotter. On all three counts, as Ortheris says, "'e didn't deserve no consideration." He was out here for three months collecting materials for a book on "Our Eastern Impedimenta," and quartering himself upon everybody, like a Cossack in evening-dress.

His particular vice — because he was a Radical, I suppose — was having garrisons
( 5 )

turned out for his inspection. He would
then dine with the officer commanding, and
insult him, across the mess-table, about the
appearance of the troops. That was Benira's
way.

He turned out troops once too often. He
came to Helanthami Cantonment on a Tues-
day. He wished to go shopping in the bazaars on Wednesday, and he " desired " the
troops to be turned out on a Thursday. On—a
—Thursday! The officer commanding could
not well refuse; for Benira was a lord. There
was an indignation meeting of subalterns in
the mess-room to call the colonel pet names.

" But the rale dimonsthrashin," says Mulvaney, " was in B Comp'ny barrick; we three
headin' it."

Mulvaney climbed on to the refreshment-
bar, settled himself comfortably by the beer,
and went on : " Whin the row was at ut's
foinest an' B Comp'ny was fur goin' out to
murthur this man Thrigg on the p'rade-
groun', Learoyd here takes up his helmut
an' sez—fwhat was ut ye said?"

" Ah said," said Learoyd, " gie us t' brass.
Tak oop a subscripshun, lads, for to put off
t' p'rade, an' if t' p'rade's not put off, ah'll
gie t' brass back agean. Thot's wot ah said.
All B Coomp'ny knawed me. Ah took oop
a big subscripshun — fower rupees eight
annas 'twas—an' ah went oot to turn t' job
over. Mulvaney an' Orth'ris coom with
me."

"We three raises the divil in couples gin'rally," explained Mulvaney.

Here Ortheris interrupted. "'Ave you read the papers?" said he.

"Sometimes," I said.

"We 'ad read the papers, an' we put hup a faked decoity, a—a sedukshun."

"*Ab*dukshun, ye cockney," said Mulvaney.

"*Ab*dukshun or sedukshun—no great odds. Any'ow, we arranged to taik an' put Mister Benhira out o' the way till Thursday was hover, or 'e too busy to rux 'isself about p'raids. Hi was the man wot said : 'We'll make a few rupees off o' the business.'"

"We hild a council av war," continued Mulvaney, "walkin' roun' by the artill'ry lines. I was prisidint, Learoyd was minister av finance, an' little Orth'ris here was—"

"A bloomin' Bismarck! Hi made the 'ole show pay."

"This interferin' bit av a Benira man," said Mulvaney, "did the thrick for us himself; for, on me sowl, we hadn't a notion av what was to come afther the next minut. He was shoppin' in the bazaar on fut. 'Twas dhrawin' dusk thin' an' we stud watchin' the little man hoppin' in an' out av the shops, thryin to injuce the naygurs to *mallum* his *bat*. Prisintly, he sthrols up, his arrums full av thruck, an' he sez in a consiquinshal way, shticking out his little belly : 'Me good men,' sez he, 'have ye seen the kernel's b'roosh?'

'B'roosh?' says Learoyd. 'There's no b'roosh here—nobbut a *hekka*.' 'Fwhat's that?' sez Thrigg. Learoyd shows him wan down the sthreet, an' he sez: 'How thruly Orientil! I will ride on a *hekka*.' I saw thin that our rigimintil saint was for givin' Thrigg over to us neck and briskit. I purshued a *hekka*, an' I sez to the dhriver-divil, I sez: 'Ye black limb, there's a sahib comin' for this hekka. He wants to go *jildi* to the Padsahi Jhil'— 'twas about tu moiles away—'to shoot snipe' —*chirria*. 'You dhrive *Jehannum ke marfik, mallum?* 'Tis no manner av *faider bukkin'* to the sahib, bekaze he doesn't *samjao* your *bat.* Av he *bolos* anything, just you *choop* and *chel. Dekker?* Go *arsty* for the first *arder*-mile from cantonmints. Then *chel, Shaitan ke marfik,* an' the *chooper* you *choops* an' the *jilder* you *chels* the better *kooshy* will that sahib be; an' here's a rupee for ye.'

"The hekka-man knew there was somethin' out av the common in the air. He grinned and sez: '*Bote achee!* I goin' damn fast.' I prayed that the kernel's b'roosh wudn't arrive till me darlin' Benira, by the grace av God, was undher way. The little man puts his thruck into the hekka an' scuttles in like a fat guinea-pig; niver offerin' us the price av a dhrink for our services in helpin' him home. 'He's off to the Padsahi Jhil,' sez I to the others." Ortheris took up the tale:

"Jist then, little Buldoo kim up, 'oo was

the son of one of the artillery *saises*—'e would
'av made a 'evinly newspaper-boy in London,
bein' sharp and fly to all manner o' games.
'E 'ad bin watchin' us puttin' Mister Benhira
into 's temporary baroush, an' 'e sez : 'What
'ave you been a-doin' of, sahibs ?' sez 'e.
Learoyd 'e caught 'im by the ear an' 'e sez—"

"Ah says," went on Learoyd : "' Young
mon, that mon's gooin' to have t' goons out
o' Thursday—*kul*—an' thot's more work for
you, young mon. Now, sitha, tak a *tat* an'
a *lookri*, an' ride tha domdest to t' Padsahi
Jhil. Cotch thot there hekka, and tell t'
driver iv your lingo thot you've coom to tak'
his place. T' sahib doesn't speak t' *bat*, an'
he's a little mon. Drive t' hekka into t' Padsahi Jhil into t' watter. Leave t' sahib theer
an' roon hoam ; an here's a rupee for tha."

Then Mulvaney and Ortheris spoke together in alternate fragments, Mulvaney
leading [You must pick out the two speakers
as best you can]: " He was a knowin' little
divil was Bhuldoo—'e sez *bote achee* an' cuts
—wid a wink in his oi—but Hi sez there's
money to be made—an' Hi want to see the
end av the campaign—so Hi says we'll double hout to the Padsahi Jhil—and save the
little man from bein' dacoited by the mur-
therin' Bhuldoo—an' turn hup like reskoors
in a Ryle Victoria Theayter melodrama—so
we doubled for the *jhil*, an' prisintly there was
the divil of a hurroosh behind us an' three
bhoys on grasscuts' *tats* come by, poundin'

along for dear life—s'elp me Bob, hif Bhuldoo 'adn't raised a regular harmy of decoits—
to do the job in shtile. An' we ran, an' they
ran, shplittin' with laughin', till we gets near
the *jhil*—and 'ears sounds of distress floatin'
molloncally on the heavenin' hair." [Or-
theris was growing poetical under the influence of the beer. The duet recommenced;
Mulvaney leading again.]

"Thin we heard Bhuldoo, the dacoit,
shoutin' to the hekka-man, an' wan of the
young divils brought his *lakri* down on the
top av the hekka-cover, an' Benira Thrigg
inside howled 'Murther an' death.' Bhuldoo
takes the reins and dhrives like mad for the
*jhil*, havin' dishpersed the hekka-dhriver
—'oo cum up to us an' 'e sez, sezie: 'That
sahib's nigh *gawbry* with funk! Wot devil's
work 'ave you led me into?' 'Hall right,'
sez we, 'you *puckrow* that there pony an'
come along. This sahib's been decoited, an'
we're going to resky 'im!' Says the driver:
'Decoits! Wot decoits? That's Bhuldoo the
*budmash* '—' Bhuldoo be shot!' sez we. ''Tis
a woild dissolute pathan frum the hills.
There's about eight av 'im coercin' the sahib.
You remimber that an' you'll get another
rupee!' Then we heard the whop-whop-
whop av the hekka turnin' over, an' a splash
ov water an' the voice av Benira Thrigg callin' upon God to forgive his sins—an' Bhuldoo
an' 'is friends squotterin' in the water like
boys in the Serpentine."

Here the three musketeers retired simultaneously into the beer.

"Well? What came next?" said I.

"Fwhat nex'?" answered Mulvaney, wiping his mouth. "Wud you let three bould sodger-bhoys lave the ornamint av the House av Lords to be dhrowned an' dacoited in a *jhil?* We formed line av quarther-column an' we desinded upon the inimy. For the better part av tin minutes you could not hear yerself spake. The tattoo was screamin' in chune wid Benira Thrigg an' Bhuldoo's army, an' the shticks was whistlin' roun' the hekka, an' Orth'ris was beatin' the hekka-cover wid his fistes, an' Learoyd yellin': 'Look out for their knives!' an' me cuttin' into the dark, right an' lef', dishpersin' arrmy corps av pathans. Holy Mother av Moses! 'twas more disp'rit than Ahmid Kheyl wid Maiwund thrown in. Afther awhile Bhuldoo an' his bhoys flees. Have ye iver seen a rale live lord thryin' to hide his nobility undher a fut an' a half av brown *jhil* wather? 'Tis the livin' image av a *bhisti's mussick* wid the shivers. It tuk toime to pershuade me frind Benira he was not disimbowiled; an' more toime to get out the hekka. The dhriver come up afther the battle, swearin' he tuk a hand in repulsin' the inimy. Benira was sick wid the fear. We escorted him back, very slow, to cantonmints, for that an' the chill to soak into him. *It suk!* Glory be to the rigimintil saint, but it suk to the marrow av Lord Benira Thrigg!"

Here Ortheris, slowly, with immense pride: "'E sez: 'You har my noble pre-servers,' sez 'e. 'You har a *honor* to the British Harmy,' sez 'e. With that 'e de-scribes the hawful band of decoits wot set on 'im. There was about forty of 'em an, 'e was hoverpowered by numbers, so 'e was; but 'e never lost 'is presence of mind, so 'e didn't. 'E guv the hekka-driver five rupees for 'is noble hassistance, an' 'e said 'e would see to us after 'e 'ad spoken to the kernul. For we was a *honor* to the regi-ment, we was."

"An' we three," said Mulvaney, with a seraphic smile, "have dhrawn the par-ti-cu-lar attinshin av Bobs Bahadur more than wanst. But he's a rale good little man is Bobs. Go on, Orth'ris, me son."

"Then we leaves 'im at the kernul's 'ouse, werry sick, an' we cuts over to B Comp'ny barrick, an' we sez we 'ave saved Benira from a bloody doom, an' the chances was agin there bein' p'raid on Thursday. About ten minutes later comes three envelicks, one for each of us. S'elp me Bob, if the old bloke 'adn't guv us a fiver apiece— sixty-four dibs in the bazaar! On Thurs-day 'e was in 'orspital recoverin' from 's sanguinary encounter with a gang of pa-thans, an' B Company was drinkin' 'em selves inter clink by squads. So there never was no Thursday p'raid. But the kernul, when 'e 'eard of our gallant conduct, 'e sez: ' Hi know there's been some devilry somewheres,' sez 'e, ' but Hi can't bring it 'ome to you three.' "

" An' my privit imprisshin is," said Mulvaney, getting off the bar and turning his glass upside down, " that, av they had known they wudn't have brought ut home. 'Tis flyin' in the face, firstly av Nature, second, av the rig'lations, an' third, the will av Terence Mulvaney, to hold p'rades av Thursdays."

" Good, ma son!" said Learoyd; " but, young mon, what's t' note-book for?"

" Let be," said Mulvaney; " this time next month we're in the 'Sherapis.' 'Tis immortal fame the gintleman's goin' to give us. But kape it dhark till we're out av the range av me little frind Bobs Bahadur."

And I have obeyed Mulvaney's order.

# THE TAKING OF LUNG-TUNGPEN.

So we loosed a bloomin' volley,
  An' we made the beggars cut,
An' when our pouch was emptied out,
  We used the bloomin' butt.
        Ho!  My!
      Don't yer come anigh,
When Tommy is a-playin' with the baynit an' the
butt.—*Barrack Room Ballad*.

My friend Private Mulvaney told me this, sitting on the parapet of the road to Dagshai, when we were hunting butterflies together. He had theories about the army, and colored clay pipes perfectly. He said that the young soldier is the best to work with, "on account av the surpassin' innocinse av the child."

"Now, listen!" said Mulvaney, throwing himself full length on the wall in the sun. "I'm a born scutt av the barrick-room! The army's mate an' dhrink to me, bekase I'm wan av the few that can't quit ut. I've put in sivinteen years, an' the pipe-clay's in the marrow av me. Av I cud have kept out av wan big dhrink a month, I wud have been a hon'ry lift'nint by this time—a nuisince to my betthers, a laughin'-shtock to my equils, an' a curse to meself. Bein'

( 14 )

fwhat I am, I'm Privit Mulvaney, wid no
good-conduc' pay an' a devourin' thirst.
Always barrin' me little frind Bobs Bahadur, I know as much about the army as
most men."

I said something here.

"Wolseley be shot! Betune you an' me
an' that butterfly net, he's a ramblin', in-
coherint sort av a divil, wid wan oi on the
quane an' the coort, an' the other on his
blessed silf—everlastin'ly playing Saysar
an' Alexandrier rowled into a lump. Now
Bobs is a sinsible little man. Wid Bobs an'
a few three-year-olds, I'd swape any army
av the earth into a *jhairun*, an' throw it
away aftherward. Faith, I'm not jokin'!
'Tis the bhoys—the raw bhoys—that don't
know fwhat a bullut manes, an' wudn't care
av they did—that dhu the work. They're
crammed wid bull-mate till they fairly *ramps*
wid good livin'; an' thin, av they don't
fight, they blow each other's hids off. 'Tis
the trut' I'm tellin' you. They shud be
kept on *dal-bhat* an' *kijri* in the hot weather;
but there'd be a mutn'y iv 'twas done.

"Did ye iver hear how Privit Mulvaney
tuk the town av Lungtungpen? I thought
not! 'Twas the lift'nint got the credit; but
'twas me planned the schame. A little before I was inviladed from Burma, me an'
four-an'-twinty young wans undher a Lift'-
nint Brazenose was ruinin' our dijeshins
thryin' to catch dacoits. An' such double-

ended divils I niver knew! 'Tis only a *dah*
an' a Snider that makes a dacoit. Widout
thim, he's a paceful cultivator, an' felony
for to shoot. We hunted, an' we hunted,
an' tuk fever an' elephints now an' again;
but no dacoits. Evenshually, we *puckarowed*
wan man. 'Trate him tinderly,' sez the
lift'nint. So I tuk him away into the jungle, wid the Burmese interprut'r an' my
clanin'-rod. Sez I to the man: ' My paceful
squireen,' sez I, ' you shquot on your hun-
kers an' dimonstrate to my frind here where
your frinds are whin they're at home?'
Wid that I introjuced him to the clanin'-
rod, and he comminst to jabber; the interprut'r interprutin' in betweens, an' me
helpin' the intilligince departmint wid my
clanin'-rod whin the man misremimbered.

"Prisintly, I learnt that, acrost the river,
about nine miles away, was a town just
dhrippin' wid dahs, an' bohs an' arrows, an'
dacoits, an' elephints, an' jingles. 'Good!'
sez I. ' This office will now close.'

"That night I went to the lift'nint an'
communicates my information. I never
thought much of Lift'nint Brazenose till
that night. He was shtiff wid books an'
the-ouries, an' all manner av thrimmin's
no manner av use. 'Town did ye say?'
sez he. 'Accordin' to the the-ouries av war,
we shud wait for reinforcemints.' 'Faith!'
thinks I, 'we'd betther dig our graves thin;'
for the nearest throops was up to their

shtocks in the marshes out Mimbu way.
'But,' says the lift'nir ., 'since 'tis a speshil
case, I'll make an excepshin. We'll visit
this Lungtungpen to-night.'

" The bhoys was fairly woild wid deloight
whin I tould 'em ; an' by this an' that, they
wint through the jungle like buck rabbits.
About midnight we come to the shtrame
which I had clane forgot to minshin to my
orficer. I was on, ahead, wid four bhoys,
an' I thought that the lift'nint might want
to the-ourize. 'Shtrip, bhoys !' sez I. 'Shtrip
to the buff, an' shwim in where glory waits !'
'But I can't shwim !' sez two av thim. 'To
think I should live to hear that from a bhoy
wid a board-school edukashin !' sez I. 'Take
a lump av timber, an' me an' Conolly here
will ferry ye over, ye young ladies !'

" We got an ould tree-trunk, an' pushed
off wid the kits an' the rifles on it. The
night was chokin' dhark, an' just as we
was fairly embarked, I heard the lift'nint
behind av me callin' out. 'There's a bit av
a *nullah* here, soor,' sez I, 'but I can feel the
bottom already.' So I cud, for I was not a
yard from the bank.

" ' Bit av a *nullah !* Bit av an eshtuary !'
sez the lift'nint. 'Go on, ye mad Irishman !
Shtrip bhoys.' I heard him laugh ; an' the
bhoys begun shtrippin' an' rollin' a log into
the wather to put their kits on. So me an'
Conolly shtruck out in the warm wather wid
our log, an' the rest come on behind.

"That shtrame was miles woide! Orth'ris, on the rear-rank log, whispers we had got into the Thames below Sheerness by mistake. 'Kape on shwimmin', ye little blayguard,' sez I, 'an' don't go pokin' your dirty jokes at the Irriwaddy.' 'Silince, men!' sings out the lift'nint. So we swum on into the black dhark, wid our chests on the logs, trustin' in the saints an' the luck av the British army.

"Evenshually we hit ground—a bit av sand—an' a man. I put my heel on the back av him. He skreeched an' ran.

"'Now we've done it!' sez Left'nint Brazenose. 'Where the divil is Lungtungpen?' There was about a minute and a half to wait. The bhoys laid a hould av their rifles an' some thried to put their belts on; we was marchin' wid fixed baynits av course. Thin we knew where Lungtungpen was; for we had hit the river-wall av it in the dhark, an' the whole town blazed wid thim messin' jingles an' Sniders like a cat's back on a frosty night. They was firin' all ways at wanst, but over our heads into the shtrame.

"'Have you got your rifles?' sez Brazenose. 'Got 'em!' sez Orth'ris. 'I've got that thief Mulvaney's for all my back pay, an' she'll kick my heart sick wid that blunderin' long shtock av hers.' 'Go on!' yells Brazenoze, whippin' his sword out. 'Go on an' take the town! An' the Lord have mercy on our sowls!'

"Thin the bhoys gave one divastatin' howl, an' pranced into the dhark, feelin' for the town, an' blindin' an' stiffinin' like cavalry ridin' masters whin the grass pricked their bare legs. I hammered wid the butt at some bamboo thing that felt wake, an' the rest come an' hammered contagious, while the jingles was jingling, an' feroshus yells from inside was sphlittin' our ears. We was too close under the wall for thim to hurt us.

"Evenshually the thing, whatever ut was, bruk; an' the six-and-twinty av us tumbled, wan afther the other, naked as we was borrun, into the town of Lungtungpen. There was a meelly av a sumpshus kind for a whoile; but whether they tuk us, all white an' wet, for a new breed av divil, or a new kind av dacoit, I don't know. They ran as though we were both, an' we wint into thim, baynit an' butt, shriekin' wid laughin'. There was torches in the sthreets, an' I saw little Orth'ris rubbin' his showlther ivry time he loosed my long-sthock Martini; an' Braze-nose walkin' into the gang wid his sword, like Diarmid av the Golden Collar—barrin' he hadn't a stitch av clothin' on him. We diskivered elephints wid dacoits under their bellies, an', what wid wan thing an' another, we was busy till mornin' takin' possession av the town of Lungtungpen.

"Thin we halted an' formed up, the wim-men howlin' in the houses an' Lift'nint Brazenose blushin' pink in the light av the mornin' sun. 'Twas the most ondasint p'rade I iver tuk a hand in. Foive-and-twinty privits an' a orficer av the line in review ordher, an' not as much as wud dust a fife betune 'em all in the way av clothin'! Eight av us had their belts an' pouches on; but the rest had gone in wid a handful av cartridges an' the skin God gave thim. They was as nakit as Vanus.

"'Number off from the right!' sez the lift'nint. 'Odd numbers fall out to dress; even numbers pathrol the town till relieved by the dressin' parthy.' Let me tell you, pathrollin' a town wid nothin' on is an ex*pay*rience. I pathrolled for tin minutes, an' begad, before 'twas over, I blushed. The women laughed so. I niver blushed before or since; but I blushed all over my carkiss thin. Orth'ris didn't pathrol. He sez only: 'Portsmith Barricks an' the 'Ard av a Sunday!' Thin he lay down an' rowled anyways wid laughin'.

"When we was all dhressed, we counted the dead—sivinty-foive dacoits, besides wounded. We tuk five elephints, a hunder' an' sivinty Sniders, two hunder' dahs, and a lot av other burglarious thruck. Not a man av us was hurt—excep' may be the lift'nint, an' he from the shock to his dasincy.

"The headman av Lungtungpen, who surrinder'd himself, asked the interprut'r: 'Av the English fight like that wid their clo'es off, what in the wurruld do they do wid their clo'es on.?' Orth'ris began rowlin' his eyes an' crackin' his fingers an' dancin' a step-dance for to impress the headman. He ran to his house; an' we spint the rest av the day carryin' the lift'nint on our showlthers round the town, an' playin' wid the Bur-mese babies—fat, little, brown little divils, as pretty as pictures.

"Whin I was inviladed for the dysent'ry to India, I sez to the lift'nint: 'Sorr,' sez I, 'you've the makin's in you av a great man; but, av you'll let an ould sodger spake, you're too fond of the-ourisin'.' He shuk hands wid me and sez: 'Hit high. hit low, there's no plasin you, Mulvaney. You've seen me waltzin' through Lungtungpen like a Red Injun widout the war paint, an' you say I'm too fond av the-ourisin'?' 'Sorr,' sez I, for I loved the bhoy, 'I wud waltz wid you in that condishin through hell, an' so wud the rest av the men!' Thin I wint down-sthrame in the flat an' left him my blessin'. May the saints carry ut where ut shud go, for he was a fine upstandin' young orficer.

"To reshume: Fhwat I've said jist shows the use av three-year-olds. Wud fifty sea-soned sodgers have taken Lungtungpen in the dhark that way? No! They'd know the risk av fever an' chill, let alone the shoot-in.' Two hunder' might have done ut. But the three-year-olds know little an' care less; an' where there's no fear, there's no danger. Catch thim young, feed thim high, an' by

the honor av that great, little man, Bobs, behind a good orficer 'tisn't only dacoits they'd
smash wid their clo'es off—'tis con-ti-
nental ar-r-r-r-mies! They tuk Lungtungpen
nakid; an' they'd take St. Pethersburg in
their dhrawers! Begad, they would that!

"Here's your pipe, sorr! Shmoke her tinderly wid honey-dew, afther letting the reek
av the canteen plug die away. But 'tis no
good, thanks to you all the same, fillin' my
pouch wid your chopped *bhoosa.* Canteen
baccy's like the army. It shpoils a man's
taste for moilder things."

So saying, Mulvaney took up his butter-
fly-net, and returned to barracks.

# THE DAUGHTER OF THE REGIMENT.

Jain 'Ardin' was a Sarjint's wife,
A Sarjint's wife wus she.
She married of 'im in Orldershort
An' comed acrost the sea.
(*Chorus*) 'Ave you never 'eard tell o' Jain 'Ardin'?
Jain 'Ardin'?
Jain 'Ardin'?
'Ave you never 'eard tell 'o Jain 'Ardin'?
The pride o' the Compan*ee*?

*Old Barrack Room Ballad.*

"A GENTLEMAN who doesn't know the Circassian circle ought not to stand up for it—puttin' everybody out." That was what Miss McKenna said, and the sergeant who was my *vis à-vis* looked the same thing. I was afraid of Miss McKenna. She was six feet high, all yellow freckles and red hair, and was simply clad in white satin shoes, a pink muslin dress, and apple-green stuff sash, and black silk gloves, with yellow roses in her hair. Wherefore I fled from Miss McKenna and sought my friend Private Mulvaney who was at the cant—refreshment-table.

"So you've been dancin' with little Jhansi McKenna, sorr—she that's goin' to marry Corp'ril Slane? Whin you next conversh wid your lorruds an' your ladies, tell thim you've danced wid little Jhansi. 'Tis a thing to be proud av."

But I wasn't proud. I was humble. I saw a story in Private Mulvaney's eye; and, besides, if he stayed too long at the bar, he would, I knew, qualify for more pack-drill. Now to meet an esteemed friend doing pack-drill outside the guard-room is embarrassing, especially if you happen to be walking with his commanding-officer.

"Come on to the parade-ground, Mulvaney, it's cooler there, and tell me about Miss McKenna. What is she, and who is she, and why is she called 'Jhansi'?"

"D'ye mane to say you've niver heard av ould Pummeloe's daughter? An' you thinkin' you know things! I'm wid ye in a minut' whin me poipe's lighted."

We came out under the stars. Mulvaney sat down on one of the artillery bridges and began in the usual way, his pipe between his teeth, his big hands clasped and dropped between his knees, and his cap well back on his head.

"Whin Mrs. Mulvaney, that is, was Miss Shad that was, you were a dale younger than you are now, an' the army was diff'rint in sev'ril e-senshuls. Bhoys have no call for to marry nowadays, an' that's why the army has so few rale, good, honust. swearin' strapagin', tinder-hearted, heavy-futted wives as ut used to have whin I was a cor'pril. I

was rejuced afterward—but no matther—I
was a cor'pril wanst. In thim times a man
lived an' died wid his rigimint; an' by natur', he married whin he was a man. Whin
I was cor'pril—Mother av Hivin, how the
rigimint has died an' been borrun since that
day—my color-sar'jint was ould McKenna,
an' a married man tu. An' his woife—his
first woife, for he married three times did
McKenna—was Bridget McKenna, from
Portarlington, like mesilf. I've misremem-
bered fwhat her first name was; but in B
Comp'ny we called her ' Ould Pummeloe '
by reason av her figure, which was entirely
cir-cum-fe-renshil. Like the big dhrum!
Now that woman—God rock her sowl to rest
in glory—was for everlastin' havin' childher; an' McKenna, whin the fifth or sixth
come squallin' on to the musther roll, swore
he wud number them off in the future. But
ould Pummeloe she prayed av him to chris-
ten thim afther the names of the stations
they was borrun in. So there was Colaba
McKenna, an' Muttra McKenna, an' a whole
presidincy av other McKennas, an' little
Jhansi, dancin' over yonder. Whin the
children wasn't bornin', they was dyin'; for,
av our childer die like sheep in these days,
they died like flies thin. I lost me own little Shad—but no matther. 'Tis long ago,
and Mrs. Mulvaney niver had another.

" I'm digresshin'. Wan divil's hot sum-
mer there come an order from some mad

ijjit, whose name I misremember, for the rigimint to go up-country. May be they wanted
to know how the new rail carried throops.
They knew! On me sowl, they knew before
they was done! Ould Pummeloe had just
buried Muttra McKenna; an' the season bein' onwholesim, only little Jhansi McKenna,
who was four years ould thin, was left on
hand.

"Five children gone in fourteen months.
'Twas harrd, wasn't ut?

"So we wint up to our new station in that
blazin' heat—may the curse av Saint Law-
rence conshume the man who gave the ordher! Will I ivir forgit that move? They
gave us two wake thrains to the rigimint; an'
we was eight hunder' and sivinty strong.
There was A, B, C an' D Comp'nies in the
secon' thrain, wid twelve women, no orficers'
ladies, an' thirteen childher. We was to go six
hunder' miles, an' railways was new in thim
days. Whin we had been a night in the
belly av the thrain—the men ragin' in their
shirts an' dhrinkin' anything they cud find,
an' eatin' bad fruitstuff whin they cud, for
we cudn't stop 'em—I was a cor'pril thin
—the cholera bruk out wid the dawnin' av
the day.

"Pray to the saints, you may niver see
cholera in a throop-thrain! 'Tis like the
judgmint av God hittin' down from the
nakid sky! We run into a rest-camp—as ut
might have been Ludianny, but not by any

means so comfortable. The orficer commandin' sent a telegrapt up the line, three hunder' mile up, askin' for help. Faith, we wanted ut, for ivry sowl av the followers ran for the dear life as soon as the thrain stopped; an' by the time that telegrapt was writ, there wasn't a naygur in the station exceptin' the telegrapt clerk—an' he only bekaze he was held down to his chair by the scruff av his sneakin' black neck. Thin the day began wid the noise in the carri'ges, an' the rattle av the men on the platform fallin' over, arms an' all, as they stud for to answer the comp'ny muster-roll before goin' over to the camp. 'Tisn't for me to say what like the cholera was like. May be the doctor cud ha' tould, av he hadn't dropped on to the platform from the door av a carri'ge where he was takin' out the dead. He died wid the rest. Some bhoys had died in the night. We tuk out sivin, an' twinty more was sickenin' as we tuk thim. The women was huddled up any ways, screamin' wid fear.

"Sez the commandin' orficer, whose name I misremember: 'Take the women over to that tope av trees yonder. Get thim out av the camp. 'Tis no place for thim.'

"Ould Pummeloe was sittin' on her beddin'-rowl, thryin' to kape little Jhansi quiet. 'Go off to that tope!' sez the orficer. 'Go out av the men's way!'

"'Be damned av I do!' sez ould Pummeloe, an' little Jhansi, squattin' by her

mother's side, squeaks out: ' Be damned av
I do,' tu. Then ould Pummeloe turns to
the women an' she sez: ' Are ye goin' to let
the bhoys die while you're picnickin', ye
sluts?' sez she. ' 'Tis wather they want.
Come on an' help.'

" Wid that, she turns up her sleeves an'
steps out for a well behind the rest-camp—
little Jhansi trottin' behind wid a *lotah* an'
string, an' the other women followin' like
lambs, wid horse-buckets and cookin' *deg-
chies.* Whin all the things was full, ould
Pummeloe marches back into camp—'twas
like a battle-field wid all the glory missin'—
at the hid av the rigimint av women.

" ' McKenna, me man !' she sez, wid a
voice on her like grand-roun's challenge,
' tell the bhoys to be quiet. Ould Pummeloe's a-comin' to look afther thim—wid
free dhrinks.'

" Thin we cheered, an' the cheerin' in
the lines was louder than the noise av
the poor divils wid the sickness on thim.
But not much.

" You see, we was a new an' raw rigimint in those days, an' we cud make
neither head nor tail av the sickness; an'
so we was useless. The men was goin'
roun' an' about like dumb sheep, waitin'
for the nex' man to fall over, an' sayin'
undher their spache: ' Fwhat is ut? In the
name av God, fwhat is ut?' 'Twas horrible.
But through ut all, up an' down, an' down

an' up, wint ould Pummeloe an' little
Jhansi—all we cud see av the baby, undher a
dead man's helmet wid the chin-strap swingin' about her little stummick—up an' down
wid the water an' fwhat brandy there was.

" Now an' thin ould Pummerloe, the tears
runnin' down her fat, red face, sez: ' Me
bhoys, me poor, dead darlin' bhoys!' But,
for the most, she was thryin' to put heart
into the men an' kape thim stiddy; an'
little Jhansi was tellin' thim all they wud
be ' betther in the mornin'.' 'Twas a thrick
she'd picked up from hearin' old Pummeloe whin Muttra was burnin' out wid
fever. In the mornin'! 'Twas the iverlastin' mornin' at St. Peter's Gate was the
mornin' for sivin-an'-twinty good men; an'
twinty more was sick to the death in that
bitter, burnin' sun. But the women worked
like angils, as I've said, an' the men like
divils, till two doctors come down from
above, an' we was rescued.

" But, just before that, ould Pummeloe,
on her knees over a bhoy in my squad—
right-cot man he was to me in the barrick—tellin' him the wurrud av the Church
that niver failed a man yet, sez : ' Hould me
up, bhoys! I'm feelin' bloody sick!' 'Twas
the sun, not the cholera, did ut. She mis-
remembered she was only wearin' her ould
black bonnet, an' she died wid ' McKenna,
me man,' houldin' her up, an' the bhoys
howled whin they buried her.

" That night, a big wind blew, an' blew, an' blew the tents flat. But it blew the cholera away, an' niver another case there was all the while we was waitin'—ten days in quarintin'. Av you will belave me, the thrack of the sickness in the camp was fur all the worruld the thrack of a man walkin' four times in a figur'-av-eight through the tents. They say 'tis the Wandherin' Jew takes the cholera wid him. I believe ut.

" An' that," said Mulvaney, illogically, " is the cause why little Jhansi McKenna is fwhat she is. She was brought up by the quarter-master sarjint's wife whin McKenna died, but she b'longs to B Comp'ny ; an' this tale I'm tellin' you—wid a proper appreciashin av Jhansi McKenna—I've belted into ivry recruity av the comp'ny as he was drafted. Faith, 'twas me belted Corp'ril Slane into askin' the gurl !"

" Not really ?"

" Man, I did ! She's no beauty to look at, but she's old Pummeloe's daughter, an' 'tis my juty to provide for her. Just before Slane got his wan-eight a day, I sez to him : ' Slane,' sez I, ' to-morrow 'twill be insubor-dinashin av me to chastise you ; but, by the sowl av ould Pummeloe, who is now in glory, av you don't give me your worrud to ask Jhansi McKenna at wanst, I'll peel the flesh off yer bones wid a brass huk to-night. 'Tis a dishgrace to B Comp'ny she's been single so long !' sez I. Was I goin' to let a three-

year-ould preshume to discoorse wid me, my
will bein' set? No! Slane wint an' asked
her. He's a good bhoy is Slane. Wan av
these days he'll get into the com'ssariat an'
dhrive a boggy wid his—savin's. So I provided for ould Pummeloe's daughter; an'
now you go along an' dance agin wid her."

And I did.

I felt a respect for Miss Jhansi McKenna;
and I went to her wedding later on.

Perhaps I will tell you about that one of
these days.

# THE GOD FROM THE MACHINE.

Hit a man an' help a woman, an' ye can't be far
wrong any ways.
*Maxims of Private Mulvaney.*

THE Inexpressibles gave a ball. They borrowed a seven-pounder from the Gunners,
and wreathed it with laurels, and made the
dancing-floor plate-glass, and provided a
supper, the like of which had never been
eaten before, and set two sentries at the door
of the room to hold the trays and programme
cards. My friend, Private Mulvaney, was
one of the sentries, because he was the tall-
est man in the regiment. When the dance
was fairly started the sentries were released,
and Private Mulvaney fled to curry favor
with the mess sergeant in charge of the supper. Whether the mess sergeant gave or
Mulvaney took, I cannot say. All that I am
certain of is that, at supper time, I found
Mulvaney with Private Ortheris, two-thirds
of a ham, a loaf of bread, half a paté de foie
gras, and two magnums of champagne, sitting on the roof of my carriage. As I came
up I heard him saying:

" Praise be a danst doesn't come as often
as ord'ly-room, or, by this an' that, Orth'ris,
me son, I wud be the dishgrace av the rig'-

mint instid av the brightest jool in uts crown."

"*Hand* the colonel's pet noosince," said Ortheris, who was a Londoner. " But wot makes you curse your rations? This 'ere fizzy stuff's good enough."

"Stuff, ye oncivilized pagin! 'Tis champagne we're dhrinkin' now. 'Tisn't that I am set ag'in. 'Tis the quare stuff wid the little bits av black leather in it. I misdoubt I will be distressin'ly sick wid it in the mornin'. Fwhat is ut?"

"Goose liver," I said, climbing on the top of the carriage, for I knew that it was better to sit out with Mulvaney than to dance many dances.

"Goose liver, is ut?" said Mulvaney. " Faith, I'm thinkin' thim that makes it wud do betther to cut up the colonel. He carries a power av liver undher his right arrum whin the days are warm an' the nights chill. He wud give thim tons an' tons av liver. 'Tis he sez so. ' I'm all liver to-day,' sez he: an' wid that he ordhers me ten days C. B for as moild a dhrink as iver a good sodger tuk betune his teeth."

"That was when 'e wanted for to wash 'isself in the fort ditch," Ortheris explained. "Said there was too much beer in the barrack water-butts for a God-fearing man. You was lucky in gittin' orf with wot you did, Mulvaney."

"You say so? Now I'm pershuaded I

3

was cruel hard trated, seein' fwhat I've done for the likes av him in the days whin my eyes were wider opin than they are now. Man alive, for the colonel to whip me on the peg in that way! Me that have saved the repitation av a ten times better man than him! 'Twas ne-farious, an' that manes a power av evil!"

"Never mind the nefariousness," I said. "Whose reputation did you save?"

"More's the pity, 'twasn't my own, but I tuk more trouble wid ut than av ut was. 'Twas just my way, messin' wid fwhat was no business av mine. Hear now!" He set-tled himself at ease on the top of the car-riage. "I'll tell you all about ut. Av coorse I will name no names, for there's wan that's an orf'cer's lady now, that was in ut, an' no more will I name places, for a man is thracked by a place."

"Eyah!" said Ortheris, lazily, "but this is a mixed story wot's comin'."

"Wanst upon a time, as the childer-books say, I was a recruity."

"Was you, though?" said Ortheris; "now that's extryordinary!"

"Orth'ris," said Mulvaney, "av you opin thim lips av yours again, I will, savin' your presince, sorr, take you by the slack av your trousers an' heave you."

"I'm mum," said Ortheris. "Wot 'ap-pened when you was a recruity?"

"I was a betther recruity than you iver

was or will be, but that's neither here nor there. Thin I became a man, an' the divil of a man I was fifteen years ago. They called me Buck Mulvaney in thim days, an', begad, I tuk a woman's eye. I did that! Ortheris, ye scrub, fwhat are ye sniggerin' at? Do you misdoubt me?"

"Divil a doubt!" said Ortheris; "but I've 'eard summat like that before."

Mulvaney dismissed the impertinence with a lofty wave of his hand and continued:

"An' the orf'cers av the rig'mint I was in in thim days was orf'cers—gran' men, wid a manner on 'em, an' a way wid 'em such as is not made these days—all but wan— wan o' the capt'ns. A bad dhrill, a wake voice, an' a limp leg—thim three things are the signs av a bad man. You bear that in your hid, Orth'ris, me son.

"An' the colonel av the rig'mint had a daughter—wan av thim lamb-like, bleatin', pick-me-up-an'-carry-me-or-I'll-die gurls such as was made for the nat'ral prey av men like the capt'n who was iverlastin' payin' coort to her, though the colonel he said time an' over, 'Kape out av the brute's way, my dear.' But he niver had the heart for to send her away from the throuble, bein' as he was a widower, an' she their wan child."

"Stop a minute, Mulvaney," said I; "how in the world did you come to know these things?"

" How did I come ?" said Mulvaney, with
a scornful grunt ; " bekase I'm turned durin'
the quane's pleasure to a lump av wood,
lookin' out straight forninst me, wid a—
a—candelabbrum in me hand, for you to
pick your cards out av, must I not see nor
feel ? Av coorse I do ! Up my back, an' in
my boots, an' in the short hair av the neck
—that's where I kape me eyes whin I'm on
duty and the reg'lar wans are fixed. Know!
Take me word for it, sorr, ivrything an' a
grate dale more is known in a rig'mint ; or
fwhat wud be the use av a mess sarjint, or
a sarjint's wife doin' wet nurse to the
major's baby ? To reshume. He was a
bad dhrill, was this capt'n—a rotten bad
dhrill—an' whin first I ran me eye over
him, I sez to myself : ' Me militia bantam !'
I sez, ' me cock av a Gosport dunghill '—
'twas from Portsmouth he came to us—
' there's combs to be cut,' sez I, ' an' by the
grace av God, 'tis Terence Mulvaney will
cut thim.'

" So he wint menowderin', an' minan-
derin', an' blandandhering roun' an' about
the colonel's daughter, an' she, poor innocint, lookin' at him like a comm'ssariat
bullock looks at the comp'ny cook. He'd
a dhirty little scrub av a black mustache,
an' he twisted an' turned ivry wurrd he
used as av he found ut too sweet for to
spit out. Eyah ! He was a tricky man an'
a liar by natur'. Some are born so. He was

wan. I knew he was over his belt in money borrowed from natives; besides a lot av other mathers which, in regard to your presince, sorr, I will oblitherate. A little av fwat I knew, the colonel knew, for he wud have none av him, an' that, I'm thinkin', by fwhat happened aftherwards, the capt'n knew.

"Wan day, bein' mortial idle, or they wud never ha' thried ut, the rig'mint gave am- shure theatricals—orf'cers an' orf'cers' ladies. You've seen the likes time an' agin, sorr, an' poor fun 'tis for them that sit in the back row an' stamp wid their boots for the honor av the rig'mint. I was told off for to shif' the scenes, haulin' up this an' draggin' down that. Light work ut was, wid lashins av beer an' the gurl that dhressed the orf'- cers' ladies . . . but she died in Aggra twelve years gone, an' my tongue's gettin' the better av me. They was actin' a play thing called 'Sweethearts,' which you may ha' heard av, an' the colonel's daughter she was a lady's-maid. The capt'n was a boy called Broom—Spread Broom was his name in the play. Thin I saw—ut come out in the actin'—fwhat I niver saw before, an' that was that he was no gentleman. They was too much together, thim two, a-whispherin' behind the scenes I shifted, an' some av what they said I heard; for I was death— blue death an' ivy—on the comb-cuttin'. He was iverlastin'ly oppressing her to fall in wid some sneakin' schame av his, an' she was thryin' to stand out ag'inst him, but not as though she was set in her will. I wonder now in thim days that my ears did not grow a yard on me head wid list'-nin'. But I looked straight forninst me, an' hauled up this, an' dragged down that, such as was my duty, an' the orf'cers' ladies sez one to another, thinkin' I was out av listen-reach: 'Fwhat an obligin' young man is this Corp'ril Mulvaney!' I was a corp'ril then. I was rejuced aftherward, but, no matther, I was a corp'ril wanst.

"Well, this 'Sweethearts' ' business wint on like most amshure theatricals, an' barrin' fwat I suspicioned, 'twasn't till the dhress-re-hearsal that I saw for certain that thim two—he the blackguard, an' she no wiser than she should ha' been—had put up an evasion."

"A what?" said I.

"E-vasion! Fwat you lorruds an' ladies call an elopement. E-vasion I calls it, be-kaze, exceptin' whin 'tis right an' natural an' proper 'tis wrong an' dhirty to steal a man's wan child not knowin' her own mind. There was a sarjint in the comm'ssariat who set my face upon e-vasions. I'll tell you about that—"

"Stick to the bloomin' captains, Mul-vaney," said Ortheris; "comm'ssariat sar-jints is low."

Mulvaney accepted the emendation and went on:

"Now, I knew that the colonel was no fool, any more than me, for I was hild the smartest man in the rig'mint, an' the colonel was the best orf'cer commandin' in Asia; so fwhat he said an' I said was a mortial truth. We knew that the capt'n was bad, but, for reasons which I have already oblitherated, I knew more than me colonel. I wud ha' rolled out his face wid the butt av me gun before permittin' av him to steal the gurl. Saints knew av he wud ha' married her, an' av he didn't she would be in great tormint, an' the divil av what you, sorr, call a 'scandal.' But I niver sthruck, niver raised me hand on me shuperior orf'cer; an' that was a merricle now I come to considher it."

"Mulvaney, the dawn's risin'," said Ortheris, "an' we're no nearer 'ome than we was at the beginnin'. Lend me your pouch. Mine's all dust."

Mulvaney pitched his pouch across, and he filled his pipe afresh.

"So the dhress-rehearsal came to an end, an', bekaze I was curious, I stayed behind whin the scene-shiftin' was ended, an' I shud ha' been in barricks, lyin' as flat as a toad under a painted cottage thing. They was talkin' in whispers, an' she was shiverin' an' gaspin' like a fresh-hukked fish. 'Are you sure you've got the hang av the manewvers?' sez he, or wurrds to that effec', as the coort-martial sez. 'Sure as death,' sez she, 'but I misdoubt 'tis cruel hard on my

father.' ' Damn your father,' sez he, or anyways 'twas fwat he thought, ' the arrangement
is as clear as mud. Jungi will drive the carri'ge afther all's over, an' you come to the
station, cool an' aisy, in time for the two-
o'clock thrain, where I will be wid your kit.'
' Faith,' thinks I to myself, ' thin there's a
ayah in the business, tu !'

"A powerful bad thing is a ayah. Don't
you niver have any thruck wid wan. Thin
he began sootherin' her, an' all the orf'cers
an' orf'cers' ladies left, an' they put out the
lights. To explain the theory av the flight, as
they say at muskthry, you must understand
that afther this ' Sweethearts' ' nonsinse was
ended there was another little bit av a play
called ' Couples '—some kind av couple or
another. The gurl was actin' in this, but not
the man. I suspicioned he'd go to the station
wid the gurl's kit at the end av the first piece.
'Twas the kit that flusthered me, for I knew for
a capt'n to go trapesing about the impire wid
the Lord knew what av a *truso* on his arrum
was nefarious, an' wud be worse than easin'
the flag, so far as the talk aftherward wint."

" ' Old on, Mulvaney. Wot's *truso* ?" said
Ortheris.

" You're an oncivilized man, me son.
Whin a gurl's married, all her kit an' 'coutrements are *truso*, which manes weddin'-
portion. An' 'tis the same whin she's runnin' away, even wid the biggest blackguard
on the arrmy list.

"So I made my plan av campaign. The colonel's house was a good two miles away. 'Dennis,' sez I to me color-sarjint, 'av you love me lend me your kyart, for me heart is bruk an' me feet is sore wid trampin' to an' from this foolishness at the Gaff' An' Dennis lent ut, wid a rampin', stampin' red stallion in the shafts. Whin they was all settled down to their 'Sweethearts' for the first scene, which was a long wan, I slips outside an' into the kyart. Mother av Hivin! but I made that horse walk, an' we came into the colonel's compound as the divil wint through Athlone—in standin' leps. There was no one there except the servints, an' I wint round to the back an' found the girl's ayah.

"'Ye black brazen Jezebel,' sez I, 'sellin' your masther's honor for five rupees—pack up all the Miss Sahib's kit an' look slippy! Capt'n Sahib's order,' sez I; 'going to the station we are,' I sez, an' wid that I laid me finger to me nose an' looked the schamin' sinner I was.

"'*Bote acchy,*' says she; so I knew she was in the business, an' I piled up all the sweet talk I'd iver learned in the bazaars on to this she-bullock, an' prayed av her to put all the quick she knew into the thing. While she packed, I stud outside an' sweated, for I was wanted for to shif' the second scene. I tell you, a young gurl's e-vasion manes as much baggage as a rig'mint on the line av march! 'Saints help Dennis's springs,' thinks I, as I bundled the stuff into the thrap, 'for I'll have no mercy!'

" 'I'm comin' too,' says the ayah.

" 'No, you don't,' sez I, 'later — *pechy!* You *baito* where you are. I'll *pechy* come an' bring you *sart*, along with me, you maraudin' '—niver mind fwhat I called her.

"Thin I wint for the Gaff, an' by the special ordher av Providence, for I was doin' a good work you will ondersthand, Dennis's springs hild toight. 'Now, whin the capt'n goes for that kit,' thinks I, 'he'll be throubled.' At the end av 'Sweethearts' off the capt'n runs in his kyart to the colonel's house, an' I sits down on the steps an' laughs. Wanst an' again I slipped in to see how the little piece was goin', an' whin ut was near endin' I stepped out all among the carri'ges an' sings out very softly, 'Jungi!' Wid that a carri'ge began to move, an' I waved to the dhriver. 'Hitherao!' sez I, an' he hitheraoed till I judged he was at proper distance, an' thin I tuk him, fair an' square betune the eyes, all I knew for good or bad, an' he dropped wid a guggle like the canteen beer-engine whin ut's runnin' low. Thin I ran to the kyart an' tuk out all the kit an' piled it into the carri'ge, the sweat runnin' down me face in dhrops. 'Go home,' sez I to the sais; 'you'll find a man close here. Very sick he is. Take him away, an' av you iver say wan wurrd about fwhat you've *dek-*

*koed*, I'll marrow you till your own wife won't *sumjao* who you are!' Thin I heard the stampin' av feet at the ind av the play, an' I ran in to let down the curtain. Whin they all came out the gurl thried to hide herself behind wan av the pillars, an' sez 'Jungi' in a voice that wudn't ha' scared a hare. I run over to Jungi's carri'ge an' tuk up the lousy old horse-blanket on the box, wrapped my head an' the rest av me in ut, an' dhrove up to where she was.

" ' Miss Sahib,' sez I ; ' goin' to the station. Captain Sahib's order!' an' widout a sign she jumped in all among her own kit.

" I laid to an' druv like steam to the colonel's house before the colonel was there, an' she screamed an' I thought she was goin' off. Out comes the ayah, sayin' all sorts av things about the capt'n havin' come for the kit an' gone to the station.

" ' Take out the luggage, you divil,' sez I, ' or I'll murther you!'

" The lights av the thraps people comin' from the Gaff was showin' acrost the parade-ground, an' by this an' that, the way thim two women worked at the bundles an' thrunks was a caution! I was dyin' to help, but, seein' I didn't want to be known, I sat wid the blanket roun' me an' coughed an' thanked the saints there was no moon that night.

" Whin all was in the house again, I niver asked for *bukshish* but druv tremenjus in the

opp'site way from the other carri'ge an' put
out me lights.   Presintly, I saw a naygur
man wallowin' in the road.  I slipped down
before I got to him, for I suspicioned Providence was wid me all through that night.
'Twas Jungi, his nose smashed in flat, all
dumb sick as you please.  Dennis's man
must have tilted him out av the thrap.
Whin he came to, ' Hutt !' sez I, but he
began to howl.

"' You black lump av dirt,' I sez, ' is this
the way you dhrive your *gharri?*   That
*tikka* has been owin' an' fereowin' all over
the bloomin' country this whole bloomin'
night, an' you as *mut-walla* as Davey's sow.
Get up, you hog!' sez I, louder, for I heard
the wheels av a thrap in the dark ; 'get up
an' light your lamps, or you'll be run into!'
This was on the road to the railway station.

"' Fwat the divil's this?' sez the capt'n's
voice in the dhark, an' I could judge he was
in a lather av rage.

"' *Gharri* dhriver here, dhrunk, sorr,' sez
I ; 'I found his *gharri* sthrayin' about cantonmints, an' now I've found him.'

"' Oh!' sez the capt'n ; 'fwhat's his name?'
I stooped down an' pretinded to listen.

"' He sez his name's Jungi, sorr,' sez I.

"' Hould my harse,' sez the capt'n to his
man, an' wid that he gets down wid the
whip an' lays into Jungi, just mad wid
rage an' swearin' like the scut he was.

" I thought, afther awhile, he wud kill the

man, so I sez, 'Stop, sir, or you'll murdher him!' That dhrew all his fire on me, an' he cursed me into blazes, an' out again. I stud to attenshin an' saluted: 'Sorr,' sez I, 'av ivry man in this worruld had his rights, I'm thinkin' that more than wan wud be beaten to a shakin' jelly for this night's work—that never came off at all, sorr, as you see.' 'Now,' thinks I to myself, 'Terence Mulvaney, you've cut your own throat, for he'll sthrike, an' you'll knock him down for the good av his sowl an' your own iverlastin' dishgrace!'

"But the capt'n never said a single wurrd. He choked where he stud, an' thin he wint into his thrap widout sayin' good-night, an' I wint back to barricks."

"And then?" said Ortheris and I together.

"That was all," said Mulvaney; "niver another wurrd did I hear av the whole thing. All I know was that there was no e-vasion, an' that was fwhat I wanted. Now, I put ut to you, sorr, is ten days' C. B. a fit an' a proper tratement for a man who has behaved as me?"

"Well, any'ow," said Ortheris, "tweren't this 'ere colonel's daughter, an' you was blazin' copped when you tried to wash in the fort ditch."

"That," said Mulvaney, finishing the champagne, "is a shuparfluous an' impert'nint observation."

# PRIVATE LEAROYD'S STORY.

And he told a tale.—*Chronicles of Guatama Buddha.*

FAR from the haunts of company officers
who insist upon kit-inspections, far from
keen-nosed sergeants who sniff the pipe
stuffed into the bedding-roll, two miles from
the tumult of the barracks, lies the Trap. It
is an old well, shadowed by a twisted pipal-
tree and fenced with high grass. Here, in
the years gone by, did Private Ortheris es-
tablish his depot and menagerie for such
possessions, living and dead, as could not
safely be introduced to the barrack-room.
Here were gathered Houdin pullets, and
fox-terriers of undoubted pedigree and more
than doubtful ownership, for Ortheris was
an inveterate poacher and pre-eminent
among a regiment of neat-handed dog-
stealers.

Never again will the long, lazy evenings
return wherein Ortheris, whistling softly,
moved surgeon-wise among the captives of
his craft at the bottom of the well; when
Learoyd sat in the niche, giving sage coun-
sel on the management of "tykes," and
Mulvaney, from the crook of the overhang-
ing pipal, waved his enormous boots in ben-

ediction above our heads, delighting us with tales of love and war, and strange experiences of cities and men.

Ortheris—landed at last in the "little stuff bird-shop" for which your soul longed; Learoyd—back again in the smoky, stone-ribbed north, amid the clang of the Bradford looms; Mulvaney—grizzled, tender, and very wise Ulysses, sweltering on the earthwork of a Central India line—judge if I have forgotten old days in the Trap!

Orth'ris as allus thinks he knaws more than other folks, said she wasn't a real laady, but nobbut a Hewrasian. I don't gainsay as her culler was a bit doosky like. But she was a laady. Why, she rode iv a carriage, an' good 'osses, too, an' her 'air was that oiled as you could see your faice in it, an' she wore di'mond rings an' a goold chain, an' silk an' satin dresses as mun 'a' cost a deal, for it isn't a cheap shop as keeps enough o' one pattern to fit a figure like hers. Her name was Mrs. De Sussa, an' t' waay I coom to be acquainted wi' her was along of our colonel's laady's dog Rip.

I've seen a vast o' dogs, but Rip was t' prettiest picter of a cliver fox-tarrier 'at iver I set eyes on. He could do owt you like but speeak, an' t' colonel's lady set more store by him than if he had been a Christian. She hed bairns of her awn, but they was i' England, and Rip seemed to get

all t' coodlin' and pettin' as belonged to a
bairn by good right.

But Rip were a bit on a rover, an' hed
a habit o' breakin' out o' barricks like, and
trottin' round t' plaice as if he were t' cantonment magistrate coom round inspectin'.
The colonel leathers him once or twice, but
Rip didn't care, an' kept on gooin' his
rounds, wi' his taail a-waggin' as if he were
flag signalin' to t' world at large 'at he was
"gettin' on nicely, thank yo', and how's
yo'sen?" An' then t' colonel, as was noa
sort of a hand wi' a dog, tees him oop. A
real clipper of a dog, an' it's noa wonder yon
laady, Mrs. De Sussa, should tek a fancy tiv
him. Theer's one o' t' Ten Commandments
says yo' maun't cuvvet your neebor's ox nor
his jackass, but it doesn't say nowt about
his tarrier-dogs, an' happen thot's t' reason
why Mrs. De Sussa cuvveted Rip, thou' she
went to church reg'lar along wi' her husband, who was so mich darker 'at if he
hedn't such a good coaat tiv his back yo'
might ha' called him a black man, and nut
tell a lee nawther. They said he addled his
brass i' jute, an' he'd a rare lot on it.

Well, you seen, when they teed Rip up, t'
oor awd lad didn't enjoy very good 'elth. So
t' colonel's laady sends for me as 'ad a naame
for bein' knowledgeable about a dog, an'
axes what's ailin' wi' him.

"Why," says I, "he's getten t' mopes, an'
what he wants is his libbaty an' coompany

like t' rest on us; wal happen a rat or two 'ud liven him oop. It's low, mum," says I, "is rats, but it's t' nature of a dog; an' soa's cuttin' round an' meetin' another dog or two an' passin' t' time o' day, an' hevvin' a bit of a turn-up w' him like a Christian."

So she says her dog maunt niver fight an' noa Christians iver fought.

"Then what's a soldier for?" says I; an' I explains to her t' contrairy qualities of a dog, 'at, when yo' coom to think on't, is one o' t' curusest things as is. For they larn to behave theirsens like gentlemen born, fit for t' fost o' coompany—they tell me t' widdy herself is fond of a good dog and knaws one when she sees it as well as onnybody; then on t' other hand a-tewin' round after cats an' gettin' mixed oop i' all manners o' blackguardly street rows, an' killin' rats, an' fightin' like divils.

T' colonel's laady says: "Well, Learoyd, I doan't agree wi' you, but you're right in a way o' speeakin', an' I should like yo' to tek Rip out a-walkin' wi' you sometimes; but yo' maunt let him fight, nor chase cats, nor do nowt 'orrid:" an' them was her very wo'ds.

Soa Rip an' me gooes out a-walkin' o' evenin's, he bein' a dog as did credit tiv a man, an' I catches a lot o' rats an' we hed a bit of a match on in an awd dry swimmin'-bath at back o' t' cantonments, an' it was none so long afore he was as bright as a but-

4

ton again. He had a way o' flyin' at them big yaller pariah dogs as if he was a harrow offan a bow, an' though his weight were nowt, he tuk 'em so suddint-like they rolled over like skittles in a halley, an' when they coot he stretched after 'em as if he were rabbit-runnin'. Saame with cats when he cud get t' cat agaate o' runnin'.

One evenin', him an' me was trespassin' ovver a compound wall after one of them mongooses 'at he'd started, an' we was busy grubbin' round a prickle-bush, an' when we looks up there was Mrs. De Sussa wi' a parasel ovver her shoulder, a-watchin' us. "Oh, my!" she sings out; "there's that lovelee dog! Would he let me stroke him, Mister Soldier?"

"Ay, he would, mum," sez I, "for he's fond o' laady's coompany. Coom here, Rip, an' speeak to this kind laady." An, Rip, seein' 'at t' moongoose hed getten clean awaay, cooms up like t' gentleman he was, nivver a hauporth shy nor okkord.

"Oh, you beautiful—you prettee dog!" she says, clippin' an' chantin' her speech in a way them sooart has o' their awn; "I would like a dog like you. You are so verree lovelee—so awfullee prettee," an' all thot sort o' talk, 'at a dog o' sense mebbe thinks nowt on, tho' he bides it by reason o' his breedin'.

An' then I meks him joomp ovver my swagger-cane, an' shek hands, an' beg, an' lie dead, an' a lot o' them tricks as laadies teeaches dogs, though I doan't haud with it mysen, for it's makin' a fool o' a good dog to do such like.

An' at lung length it cooms out 'at she'd been thrawin' sheep's eyes, as t' sayin' is, at Rip for many a day. Yo' see, her childer was grown up, an' she'd nowt mich to do, an' were allus fond of a dog. Soa she axes me if I'd tek somethin' to dhrink. An' we goes into t' drawn room wheer her 'usband was a-settin'. They meks a gurt fuss ovver t' dog an' I has a bottle o' aale an' he gave me a handful o' cigars.

Soa I coomed away, but t' awd lass sings out: "Oh, Mister Soldier! please coom again and bring that prettee dog."

I didn't let on to t' colonel's laady about Mrs. De Sussa, and Rip, he says nowt nawther; an' I gooes again, an' ivry time there was a good dhrink an' a handful o' good smooaks. An' I telled t' awd lass a heeap more about Rip than I'd ever heeared; how he tuk t' fost prize at Lunnon dog-show and cost thotty-three pounds fower shillin' from t' man as bred him; 'at his own brother was t' proputty o' t' Prince o' Wailes, an' 'at he had a pedigree as long as a dook's. An' she lapped it all oop an' were niver tired o' admirin' him. But when t' awd lass took to givin' me money an' I seed 'at she were gettin' fair fond about t' dog, I began to suspicion summat. Onnybody may give a

soldier t' price of a pint in a friendly way
an' theer's no 'arm done, but when it cooms
to five rupees slipt into your hand, sly like,
why, it's what t' 'lectioneerin' fellows calls
bribery an' corruption. Specially when Mrs.
De Sussa threwed hints how t' cold weather
would soon be ovver an' she was goin' to
Munsooree Pahar, an' we was goin' to Rawal-
pindi, an' she would never see Rip any more
onless somebody she knowed on would be
kind tiv her.

Soa I tells Mulvaney an' Ortheris all t'
taale thro', beginnin' to end.

"'Tis larceny that wicked ould lady
manes," says t' Irishman, "'tis felony she
is sejuicin' ye into, me friend Learoyd, but
I'll purtect your innocince. I'll save ye
from the wicked wiles av that wealthy ould
woman, an' I'll go wid you this evenin' an'
spake to her the wurrds av truth an' honesty. But Jock," says he, waggin' his heead,
"'twas not like ye to kape all that good
dhrink an' thim fine cigars to yerself, while
Orth'ris here an' me have been prowlin'
round wid throats as dry as lime-kilns,
an' nothin' to smoke but canteen plug.
'Twas a dhirty thrick to play on a comrade,
for why should you, Learoyd, be balancin'
yourself on the butt av a satin chair, as
if Terence Mulvaney was not the aquil av
anybody who thrades in jute!"

"Let alone me," sticks in Orth'ris; "but
that's like life. Them wot's really fitted to

decorate society get no show, while a blun-
derin' Yorkshireman like you—"

" Nay," says I, " It's none o' t' blunderin'
Yorkshireman she wants, it's Rip. He's t'
gentleman this journey."

Soa t' next day, Mulvaney an' Rip an' me
goes to Mrs. De Sussa's, an' t' Irishman bein'
a strainger she wor a bit shy at fost. But
you've heeard Mulvaney talk, an' yo' may
believe as he fairly bewitched t' awd lass
wal she let out 'at she wanted to tek Rip
away wi' her to Munsooree Pahar. Then
Mulvaney changes his tune an' axes her
solemn-like if she'd thought o' t' conse-
quences o' gettin' two poor but honest soldiers sent t' Andamning Islands. Mrs. De
Sussa began to cry, so Mulvaney turns round
oppen t' other tack and smooths her down,
allowin' 'at Rip ud be a vast better off in t'
hills than down i' Bengal, an' 'twas a pity
he shouldn't go wheer he was so well be-
liked. And soa he went on, backin' an'
fillin' an' workin' up t' awd lass wal she felt
as if her life warn't worth nowt if she didn't
hev t' dog.

Then all of a suddint he says: "But ye
shall have him, marm, for I've a feelin'
heart, not like this cowld-blooded Yorkshireman ; but 'twill cost ye not a penny less than
three hundher rupees."

"Don't you's believe him, mum," says I ;
" t' colonel's laady wouldn't tek five hundred
for him."

"Who said she would?" says Mulvaney; "it's not buyin' him I mane, but for the sake o' this kind, good laady, I'll do what I never dreamt to do in my life. I'll stale him!"

"Don't say steal," says Mrs. De Sussa; "he shall have the happiest home. Dogs often get lost, you know, and then they stray, an' he likes me, and I like him as I niver liked a dog yet, an' I must hev him. If I got him at t' last minute I could carry him off to Munsooree Pahar and nobody would niver knaw."

Now an' again Mulvaney looked acrost at me, an' though I could mak nowt o' what he was after, I concluded to take his leead.

"Well, mum," I says, "I never thowt to coom down to dog-stealin', but if my comrade sees how it could be done to oblige a laady like yo'sen, I'm nut t' man to hod back, tho' it's a bad business, I'm thinkin', an' three hundred rupees is a poor set-off again t' chance of them Damning Islands as Mulvaney talks on."

"I'll mek it three fifty," says Mrs. De Sussa; "only let me hev t' dog!"

So we let her persuade us, an' she teks Rip's measure theer an' then, an' sent to Hamilton's to order a silver collar again t' time when he was to be her awn, which was to be t' day she set off for Monsooree Pahar.

"Sitha, Mulvaney," says I, when we was outside, "you're niver goin' to let her hev Rip!"

"An' would ye disappoint a poor ould woman?" says he; "she shall have *a* Rip."

"An' wheer's he to come through?" says I.

"Learoyd, me man," he sings out, "you're a pretty man av your inches an' a good comrade, but your head is made av duff. Isn't our friend Orth'ris a taxidermist, an' a rale artist wid his nimble white fingers! An' what's a taxidermist but a man who can thrate skins? Do ye mind the white dog that belongs to the canteen sarjint, bad cess to him—he that's lost half his time an' snarlin' the rest? He shall be lost for good now; an' do ye mind that he's the very spit in shape an' size av the colonel's, barrin' that his tail is an inch too long, an' he has none av the color that divarsifies the rale Rip, an' his timper is that av his masther an' worse. But fwhat is an inch on a dog's tail? An' fwhat to a professional like Orth'ris is a few ring-straked shpots av black, brown, an' white? Nothin' at all, at all."

Then we meets Orth'ris, an' that little man, bein' sharp as a needle, seed his way through t' business in a minute. An' he went to work a-practicin' 'air-dyes the very next day, beginnin' on some white rabbits he had, an' then he drored all Rip's markin's on t' back of a white commissariat bullock, so as to get his 'and in an' be sure of his colors; shadin' off brown into black as na-teral as life. If Rip had a fault it was too mich markin', but it was straingely reg'lar,

an' Orth'ris settled himself to make a fost-
rate job on it when he got haud o' t' canteen
sarjint's dog. Theer niver was sich a dog as
thot for bad temper, an' it did nut get no
better when his tail hed to be fettled an' inch
an' a half shorter. But they may talk o' theer
Royal Academies as they like, I niver seed a
bit o' animal paintin' to beat t' copy as
Orth'ris made of Rip's marks, wal t' picter
itself was snarlin' all t' time an' tryin' to get
at Rip standin' theer to be copied as good as
goold

Orth'ris allus hed as mich conceit on him-
sen as would lift a balloon, an' he wor so
pleeased wi' his sham Rip he wor for tek-
kin' him to Mrs. De Sussa before she went
away. But Mulvaney an' me stopped thot,
knowin' Orth'ris's work, though niver so
cliver, was nobbut skin-deep. An' at last
Mrs. De Sussa fixed t' day for startin' to
Munsooree Pahar. We was to tek Rip to t'
stayshun i' a basket an' hand him ovver just
when they was ready to start, an' then she'd
give us t' brass—as was agreed upon.

An' my wo'd! It were high time she were
off, for them 'air-dyes on t' cur's back took a
vast of paintin' to keep t' reet culler, tho'
Orth'ris spent a matter of seven rupees six
annas i' t' best drooggist shops i' Calcutta.

An' t' canteen sarjint was lookin' for 'is
dog everywheer; an', wi' bein' tied up, t'
beast's timper got waur nor ever.

It wor i' t' evenin' when t' train started

thro' Howrah, an' we 'elped Mrs. De Sussa
wi' about sixty boxes, an' then we gave
her t' basket. Orth'ris, for pride av his
work, axed us to let him coom along wi' us,
an' he couldn't help liftin' t' lid an' showin'
t' cur as he lay coiled oop.

"Oh!" says t' awd lass; "the beautee!
How sweet he looks!" An' just then t'
beauty snarled an' showed his teeth, so Mulvaney shuts down t' lid and says: "Ye'll be
careful, marm, whin ye tek him out. He's
disaccustomed to traveling by t' railway, an'
he'll be sure to want his rale mistress an' his
friend Learoyd, so ye'll make allowance for
his feelings at fost."

She would do all thot an' more for the
dear, good Rip, an' she would nut oppen t'
basket till they were miles away, for fear
anybody should recognize him, an' we were
real good an' kind soldier-men, we were, an'
she honds me a bundle o' notes, an' then
cooms up a few of her relations an' friends
to say good-bye—not more than seventy-five
there wasn't—an' we cuts away.

What coom t' three hundred an' fifty rupees? Thot's what I can scarcelins tell you,
but we melted it. It was share an' share
alike, for Mulvaney said: "If Learoyd got
hold of Mrs. De Sussa first, sure 'twas I that
remimbered the sarjint's dog just in the nick
av time, an' Orth'ris was the artist av janius
that made a work av art out av that ugly
piece av ill-nature. Yet, by way av a thank-

offerin' that I was not led into felony by that wicked ould woman, I'll send a thrifle to Father Victor for the poor people he's always beggin' for."

But me an' Orth'ris, he bein' cockney an' I bein' pretty far north, did nut see it in t' saame way. We'd getten t' brass, an' we meaned to keep it. An' soa we did—for a short time.

Noa, noa, we niver heeard a wod more o' t' awd lass. Our rig'mint went to Pindi, an' t' canteen sarjint he got himself another tyke insteead o' t' one 'at got lost so reg'lar, an' was lost for good at last.

# THE MADNESS OF PRIVATE ORTHERIS.

Oh ! Where would I be when my froat was dry?
Oh ! Where would I be when the bullets fly?
Oh ! Where would I be when I come to die?
             Why,
Somewheres anigh my chum.
  If 'e's liquor 'e'll give me some,
  If I'm dyin' 'e'll 'old my 'ead,
  An' 'e'll write 'em 'Ome when I'm dead.—
Gawd send us a trusty chum !
              *Barrack Room Ballad.*

My friends Mulvaney and Ortheris had gone on a shooting expedition for one day. Learoyd was still in hospital, recovering from fever picked up in Burma. They sent me an invitation to join them, and were genuinely pained when I brought beer—almost enough beer to satisfy two privates of the line—and me.

"'Twasn't for that we bid you welkim, sorr," said Mulvaney, sulkily. "'Twas for the pleasure av your comp'ny."

Ortheris came to the rescue with : "Well, 'e won't be none the worse for bringin' liquor with 'm. We ain't a file o' dooks. We're bloomin' Tommies, ye cantankris Hirishman ; an' 'ere's your very good 'ealth !"

We shot all the forenoon, and killed two pariah-dogs, four green parrots, sitting, one kite by the burning-ghaut, one snake flying, one mud-turtle, and eight crows. Game was plentiful. Then we sat down to tiffin— "bull-mate an' bran-bread," Mulvaney called it—by the side of the river, and took pot shots at the crocodiles in the intervals of cutting up the food with our only pocket-knife. Then we drank up all the beer, and threw the bottles into the water and fired at them. After that, we eased belts and stretched ourselves on the warm sand and smoked. We were too lazy to continue shooting.

Ortheris heaved a big sigh as he lay on his stomach with his head between his fists. Then he swore quietly into the blue sky.

"Fwhat's that for?" said Mulvaney. "Have ye not drunk enough?"

"Tott'nim Court Road, an' a gal I fancied there. Wot's the good of sodgerin'?"

"Orth'ris, me son," said Mulvaney, hastily, "'tis more than likely you've got throuble in your inside with the beer. I feel that way mesilf whin my liver gets rusty."

Ortheris went on slowly, not heeding the interruption:

"I'm a Tommy—a bloomin', eight-anna, dog-stealin' Tommy, with a number instead o' a decent name. Wot's the good o' me? If I 'ad a stayed at 'ome, I might a' married that gal an' kep' a little shorp in the 'Am-

mersmith Igh—'S. Orth'ris, Prac-ti-cal Taxi-
der-mist.' With a stuff' fox, like they 'as
in the Haylesbury Dairies, in the winder, an'
a little case of blue an' yaller glass heyes,
an' a little wife to call 'shorp!' 'shorp!'
when the door bell rung. As it his, I'm on'y
a Tommy—a bloomin', Gawdforsaken, beer-
swillin' Tommy. 'Rest on your harms—
'versed. Stan' at—hease.' Shun. 'Verse—
harms. Right an' lef' tarrn. Slow—march.
'Alt—front. Rest on your harms—'versed.
With blank cartridge—load.' An' that's the
end o' me." He was quoting fragments from
Funeral Parties' Orders.

"Stop ut!" shouted Mulvaney. "Whin
you've fired into nothin' as often as me, over
a better man than yoursilf, you will not
make a mock av thim orders. 'Tis worse
than whistlin' the 'Dead March' in barricks.
An' you full as a tick, an' the sun cool, an'
all an' all! I take shame for you. You're
no better than a pagin—you an' your firin'
parties an' your glass eyes. Won't you stop
ut, sorr?"

What could I do? Could I tell Ortheris
anything that he did not know of the pleas-
ures of his life? I was not a chaplain nor
a subaltern, and Ortheris had a right to speak
as he thought fit.

"Let him run, Mulvaney," I said. "It's
the beer."

"No! 'Tisn't the beer," said Mulvaney.
"I know fwhat's comin'. He's tuk this way

now an' ag'in, an' it's bad—it's bad—for I'm
fond av the bhoy."

Indeed, Mulvany seemed needlessly anxious; but I knew that he looked after Orth'-
ris in a fatherly way.

"Let me talk, let me talk," said Ortheris,
dreamily. "D' you stop your parrit screamin' of a 'ot day, when the cage is a-cookin'
'is pore little pink toes orf, Mulvaney?"

"Pink toes! D'ye mane to say you've
pink toes under your bullswools, ye blan-
danderin' "—Mulvaney gathered himself together for a terrific denunciation—"school-
misthress! Pink toes! How much Bass wid
the label did that ravin' child dhrink?"

"'Tain't Bass," said Ortheris. "It's a bit-
terer beer nor that. It's 'ome sickness!"

"Hark to him! An' he's goin' home
in the 'Sherapis' in the inside av four
months!"

"I don't care. It's all one to me. 'Ow d' you
know I ain't 'fraid o' dyin' 'fore I gets my
papers?" He recommenced, in a sing-song
voice, the Funeral Orders.

I had never seen this side of Ortheris's
character before, but evidently Mulvaney
had, and attached serious importance to it.
While Ortheris babbled, with his head on
his arms, Mulvaney whispered to me:

"He's always tuk this way whin he's been
checked overmuch by the childher they
make sarjints nowadays. That an' havin'
nothin' to do. I can't make ut out any ways."

" Well, what does it matter? Let him talk himself through."

Ortheris began singing a parody of " The Ramrod Corps," full of cheerful allusions to battle, murder, and sudden death. He looked out across the river as he sung, and his face was quite strange to me. Mulvaney caught me by the elbow to insure attention.

" Matther? It matthers everything! 'Tis some sort av fit that's on him. I've seen ut. 'T will hould him all this night, an' in the middle av it he'll get out av his cot an' go rakin' in the rack for his 'coutrements. Thin he'll come over to me an' say : ' I'm goin' to Bombay. Answer for me in the mornin'.' Thin me an' him will fight as we've done before— him to go an' me to hould him—an' so we'll both come on the books for disturbin' in barricks. I've belted him, an' I've bruk his head, an' I've talked to him, but 'tis no manner av use whin the fit's on him. He's as good a bhoy as ever stepped whin his mind's clear. I know fwhat's comin', though, this night in barricks. Lord send he doesn't loose off whin I rise for to knock him down. 'Tis that that's in me mind day an' night."

This put the case in a much less pleasant light, and fully accounted for Mulvaney's anxiety. He seemed to be trying to coax Ortheris out of the " fit;" for he shouted down the bank where the boy was lying:

" Listen, now, you wid the ' pore pink toes ' an' the glass eyes! Did you shwim the Irri-

waddy at night, behin' me, as a bhoy shud;
or were you hidin' under a bed, as you was
at Ahmed Kheyl?"

This was at once a gross insult and a direct
lie, and Mulvaney meant it to bring on a
fight. But Ortheris seemed shut up in some
sort of trance. He answered slowly, without a sign of irritation, in the same cadenced
voice as he had used for his firing-party orders:

" Hi swum the Irriwaddy in the night, as
you know, for to take the town Lungtungpen, nakid an' without fear. Hand where I
was at Ahmed Kheyl you know, and four
bloomin' Pathans know too. But that was
summat to do, an' I didn't think o' dyin'.
Now I'm sick to go 'ome—go 'ome—go 'ome!
No, I ain't mammy sick, because my uncle
brung me up, but I'm sick for London
again; sick for the sounds of 'er, an' the
sights of 'er, an' the stinks of 'er; orange-
peel an' hasphalt an' gas comin' in over
Vaux'all Bridge. Sick for the rail goin'
down to Box 'Ill, with your gal on your
knee an' a new clay pipe in your face. That,
an' the Stran' lights where you knows
ev'ry one, an' the copper that takes you up
is a old friend that tuk you up before, when
you was a little smitchy boy lyin' loose
'twen the Temple an' the Dark Harches.
No bloomin' guard-mountin', no bloomin'
rotten-stone, nor khaki, an' yourself your
own master with a gal to take an' see the

Humaners practicin' a-hookin' dead corpses out o' the Serpentine o' Sundays. An' I lef' all that for to serve the widder beyond the seas where there ain't no women an' there ain't no liquor worth 'avin', an' there ain't nothin' to see, nor do, nor say, nor feel, nor think. Lord love you, Stanley Orth'ris, but you're a bigger bloomin' fool than the rest o' the rig'mint an' Mulvaney wired together! There's the widder sittin' at 'ome with a gold crown on 'er 'ead ; an' 'ere Hi, Stanley Orth'ris, the widder's property, a rottin' FOOL !"

His voice rose at the end of the sentence, and he wound up with a six-shot Anglo-vernacular oath. Mulvaney said nothing, but looked at me as if he expected that I could bring peace to poor Ortheris's troubled brain.

I remembered once at Rawal Pindi having seen a man, nearly mad with drink, sobered by being made fool of. Some regiments may know what I mean. I hoped that we might shake off Ortheris in the same way, though he was perfectly sober ; so I said :

"What's the use of grousing there, and speaking against the widow ?"

" I didn't !" said Ortheris. "S'elp me Gawd, I never said a word agin 'er, an' I wouldn't—not if I was to desert this minute !"

Here was my opening. " Well, you meant to, anyhow. What's the use of cracking on for nothing? Would you slip it now if you got the chance?"

"On'y try me!" said Ortheris, jumping to his feet as if he had been stung.

Mulvaney jumped too. "Fwhat are you goin' to do?" said he.

"Help Ortheris down to Bombay or Karachi, whichever he likes. You can report that he separated from you before tiffin, and left his gun on the bank here!"

"I'm to report that—am I?" said Mulvaney, slowly. "Very well. If Orth'ris manes to desert now, an' will desert now, an' you, sorr, who have been a friend to me an' to him, will help him to ut, I, Terence Mulvaney, on my oath, which I've never bruk yet, will report as you say. But"— here he stepped up to Ortheris, and shook the stock of the fowling-piece in his face— "your fistes help you, Stanley Orth'ris, if iver I come across you agin!"

"I don't care!" said Ortheris. "I'm sick o' this dorg's life. Give me a chanst. Don't play with me. Le' me go!"

"Strip," said I, "and change with me, and then I'll tell you what to do."

I hoped that the absurdity of this would check Ortheris, but he had kicked off his ammunition-boots and got rid of his tunic almost before I had loosed my shirt-collar. Mulvaney gripped me by the arm:

"The fit's on him; the fit's workin' on him still. By my honor an' sowl, we shall

be accessiry to a desartion yet; only twinty-
eight days, as you say, sorr, or fifty-six, but
think o' the shame—the black shame to him
an' me!" I had never seen Mulvaney so
excited.

But Ortheris was quite calm, and as soon
as he had exchanged clothes with me, and I
stood up a private of the line, he said
shortly: "Now! Come on. What nex'?
D'ye mean fair? What must I do to get out
o' this 'ere hell?"

I told him that if he would wait for two or
three hours near the river I would ride into
the station and come back with one hundred rupees. He would, with that money in
his pocket, walk to the nearest side-station
on the line, about five miles away, and
would there take a first-class ticket for Karachi. Knowing that he had no money on
him when he went out shooting, his regiment would not immediately wire to the
sea-ports, but would hunt for him in the
native villages near the river. Further, no
one would think of seeking a deserter in a
first-class carriage. At Karachi he was to
buy white clothes and ship, if he could, on a
cargo-steamer.

Here he broke in. If I helped him to
Karachi he would arrange all the rest. Then
I ordered him to wait where he was until it
was dark enough for me to ride into the sta-
tion without my dress being noticed. Now
God in His wisdom has made the heart of a

British soldier, who is very often an un-
licked ruffian, as soft as the heart of a little
child, in order that he may believe in and
follow his officers into tight and nasty
places. He does not so readily come to believe in a "civilian," but, when he does, he
believes implicitly and like a dog. I had
had the honor of the friendship of Private
Ortheris, at intervals, for more than three
years, and we had dealt with each other as
man by man. Consequently, he considered
that all my words were true, and not spoken
lightly.

Mulvaney and I left him in the high grass
near the river bank, and went away, still
keeping to the high grass, toward my horse.
The shirt scratched me horribly.

We waited nearly two hours for the dusk
to fall and allow me to ride off. We spoke
of Ortheris in whispers, and strained our ears
to catch any sound from the spot where we
had left him. But we heard nothing except
the wind in the plume-grass.

"I've bruk his head," said Mulvaney,
earnestly, "time an' agin. I've nearly kilt
him wid the belt, an' yet I can't knock thim
fits out ov his soft head. No! An' he's not
soft, for he's reasonable an' likely by natur'.
Fwhat is ut? Is ut his breedin', which is
nothin', or his edukashin, which he niver
got? You that think ye know things, answer me that."

But I found no answer. I was wondering

how long Ortheris, on the bank of the river,
would hold out, and whether I should be
forced to help him to desert, as I had given
my word.

Just as the dusk shut down and, with a
very heavy heart. I was beginning to saddle
up my horse, we heard wild shouts from the
river.

The devils had departed from Private
Stanley Ortheris, No. 22639, B Company.
The loneliness, the dusk, and the waiting
had driven them out as I had hoped. We
set off at the double and found him plung-
ing about wildly through the grass, with his
coat off—my coat off, I mean. He was call-
ing for us like a madman.

When we reached him he was dripping
with perspiration and trembling like a star-
tled horse. We had great difficulty in sooth-
ing him. He complained that he was in
civilian kit, and wanted to tear my clothes
off his body. I ordered him to strip, and
we made a second exchange as quickly as
possible.

The rasp of his own "grayback" shirt and
the squeak of his boots seemed to bring him
to himself. He put his hands before his
eyes and said:

"Wot was it? I 'ain't mad, I ain't sunstrook, an' I've bin an' gone an' said, an' bin
an' gone an' done. . . Wot 'ave I bin an'
done?"

"Fwhat have you done?" said Mulvaney.

" You've dishgraced yourself—though that's no matter.    You've dishgraced B Comp'ny, an' worst av all, you've dishgraced me.    Me that taught you how for to walk abroad like a man—whin you was a dhirty little, fish-backed little, whimperin' little recruity.    As you are now, Stanley Orth'ris !"

Ortheris said nothing for awhile.    Then he unslung his belt, heavy with the badges of half a dozen regiments that his own had lain with, and handed it over to Mulvaney.

" I'm too little for to mill you, Mulvaney," said he, " an' you've strook me before ; but you can take an' cut me in two with this 'ere if you like."

Mulvaney turned to me.

" Lave me talk to him, sorr," said Mulvaney.

I left, and on my way home thought a good deal over Ortheris in particular, and my friend, Private Thomas Atkins, whom I love, in general.

But I could not come to any conclusion of any kind whatever.

# THE SOLID MULDOON.

Did you see John Malone, wid his shinin', brand-new
    hat?
Did ye see how he walked like a grand aristocrat?
There was flags an' banners wavin' high, an' dhress
    and shtyle were shown,
But the best av all the company was Misther John
    Malone.

*John Malone.*

This befell in the old days, and, as my
friend Private Mulvaney was specially careful to make clear, the Unregenerate.

There had been a royal dog-fight in the
ravine at the back of the rifle-butts between
Learoyd's Jock and Ortheris's Blue Rot—
both mongrel Rampur hounds, chiefly ribs
and teeth. It lasted for twenty happy, howling minutes, and then Blue Rot collapsed
and Ortheris paid Learoyd three rupees, and
we were all very thirsty. A dog-fight is a
most heating entertainment, quite apart
from the shouting, because Rampurs fight
over a couple of acres of ground. Later,
when the sound of belt-badges clinking
against the necks of beer-bottles had died
away, conversation drifted from dog to man
fights of all kinds. Humans resemble red-
deer in some respects. Any talk of fighting
seems to wake up a sort of imp in their

breasts, and they bell one to the other, exactly like challenging bucks. This is noticeable even in men who consider themselves superior to privates in the line; it shows the refining influence of civilization and the march of progress.

Tale provoked tale, and each tale more beer. Even dreamy Learoyd's eyes began to brighten, and he unburdened himself of a long history in which a trip to Malham Cove, a girl at Pateley Brigg, a ganger, himself and a pair of clogs were mixed in drawling tangle.

"An' so Ah coot's yead oppen from t' chin to t' hair an' he was abed for t' matter o' a month," concluded Learoyd, pensively.

Mulvaney came out of a reverie—he was lying down—and flourished his heels in the air. "You're a man, Learoyd," said he, critically, "but you've only fought wid men, an' that's an ivry-day expayrience; but I've stud up to a ghost, an' that was not an ivry-day expayrience."

"No?" said Ortheris, throwing a cork at him. "You git up an' address the 'ouse— you an' yer expayriences. Is it a bigger one nor usual?"

"'Twas the livin' trut'!" answered Mulvaney, stretching out a huge arm and catching Ortheris by the collar. "Now where are ye, me son? Will ye take the wurrud av the Lorrd out av my mout another time?" He shook him to emphasize the question.

"No, somethin' else, though," said Orthe-ris, making a dash at Mulvaney's pipe, cap-turing it, and holding it at arm's-length; I'll chuck it acrost the ditch if you don't let me go!"

"You maraudin' hathen! 'Tis the only cutty I iver loved. Handle her tinder, or I'll chuck you acrost the nullah. If that poipe was bruk— Ah! Give her back to me, sorr!"

Ortheris had passed the treasure to my hand. It was an absolutely perfect clay, as shiny as the black ball at pool. I took it reverently, but I was firm.

"Will you tell us about the ghost-fight if I do?" I said.

"Is ut the shtory that's troublin' you? Av course I will. I mint to all along. I was only gettin' at ut my own way, as Popp Doggle said whin they found him thrying to ram a cartridge down the muzzle. Orth'ris, fall away!"

He released the little Londoner, took back his pipe, filled it, and his eyes twinkled. He has the most eloquent eyes of any one that I know.

"Did I iver tell you," he began, "that I was wanst the divil av a man?"

"You did," said Learoyd, with a childish gravity that made Ortheris yell with laugh ter, for Mulvaney was always impressing upon us his merits in the old days.

"Did I iver tell you," Mulvaney continued

calmly, "that I was wanst more av a divil than I am now?"

"Mer—ria! You don't mean it?" said Ortheris.

"Whin I was corp'ril—I was rejuced afterwards—but, as I say, whin I was corp'ril, I was a divil of a man."

He was silent for nearly a minute, while his mind rummaged among old memories and his eye glowed. He bit upon the pipe-stem and charged into his tale.

"Eyah! They was great times. I'm ould now; me hide's wore off in patches; sinthry-go has disconceited me, an' I'm a married man tu. But I've had my day, I've had my day, an' nothin' can take away the taste av that! Oh, my time past, whin I put me fut through ivry livin' wan av the Tin Commandmints between revelly an' lights out, blew the froth off the pewter, wiped me mustache wid the back av me hand, an' slept on ut all as quiet as a little child! But ut's over—ut's over, an' 'twill niver come back to me; not though I prayed for a week av Sundays. Was there any wan in the ould rig'mint to touch Corp'ril Terence Mulvaney whin that same was turned out for sedukshin? I niver met him. Ivry woman that was not a witch was worth the runnin' afther in those days, an' ivry man was my dearest friend or—I had stripped to him an' we knew which was the better av the tu.

"Whin I was corp'ril I wud not ha'

changed wid the colonel—no, nor yet the commander-in-chief. I wud be a sarjint. There was nuthin' I wud not be! Mother av Hivin, look at me! Fwhat am I now? But no matther! I must get to the other ghosts—not the ones in my ould head.

"We was quartered in a big cantonmint —'tis no manner av use namin' names, fur ut might give the barricks disrepitation—an' I was the imperor av the earth to me own mind, an' wan or tu women thought the same. Small blame to thim. Afther we had lain there a year, Bragin, the color-sarjint av E Comp'ny, wint an' took a wife that was lady's-maid to some big lady in the station. She's dead now, is Annie Bragin—died in child-bed at Kirpa Tal, or ut may ha' been Almorah — siven — nine years agone, an' Bragin he married ag'in. But she was a pretty woman whin Bragin inthrojuced her to cantonmint society. She had eyes like the brown av a buttherfly's wing whin the sun catches ut, an' a waist no thicker than me arm, an' a little sof' button av a mout' I would ha' gone through all Asia bristlin' wid bay'nits to get the kiss av. An' her hair was as long as the tail av the colonel's charger—forgive me mintionin' that blun-derin' baste in the same mouthful wid Annie Bragin—but 'twas all shpun gold, an' time was whin a lock av ut was more than di'monds to me. There was niver pretty woman yet, an' I've had thruck wid a few, cud open the door to Annie Bragin.

" 'Twas in the Carth'lic chapel I saw her first, me oi rollin' round as usual to see fwhat was to be seen. ' You're too good for Bragin, me love,' thinks I to meself, ' but that's a mistake I can put straight, or me name is not Terence Mulvaney.'

" Now take my wurrd for ut, you Orth'ris there an' Learoyd, an' kape out av the married quarters—as I did not. No good iver comes av ut, an' there's always the chance av your bein' found wid your face in the dirt, a long picket in the back av your head, an' your hands playing the fifes on the tread av another man's doorstep. 'Twas so we found O'Hara, he that Rafferty killed six years gone, when he wint to his death wid his hair oiled, whistlin' ' Billy O'Rourke' betune his teeth. Kape out av the married quarters, I say, as I did not. 'Tis onwholesim, 'tis dangerous, an' 'tis ivrything else that's bad, but— Oh, my sowl, 'tis swate while it lasts!

" I was always hangin' about there whin I was off duty an' Bragin wasn't, but niver a sweet word beyon' ordinar' did I get from Annie Bragin. ''Tis the pervarsity av the sect,' sez I to mesilf, an' gave me cap another cock on me head an' straightened me back—'twas the back av a dhrum-major in those days—an' wint off as tho' I did not care, wid all the women in the married quar-

ters laughin'. I was pershuaded—most bhoys
are, I'm thinkin'—that no woman born av
woman cud stand against me av I hild up
me little finger. I had reason for thinkin'
that way—till I met Annie Bragin.

"Time an' ag'in whin I was blanhanderin'
in the dusk a man would go past me as quiet
as a cat. 'That's quare,' thinks I, 'for I
am, or I should be, the only man in these
parts. Now what divilment can Annie be
up to?' Thin I called meself a blayguard
for thinkin' such things; but I thought thim
all the same. An' that, mark you, is the
way av a man.

"Wan evenin' I said: 'Mrs. Bragin, manin' no disrespect to you, who is that cor-
p'ril man'—I had seen the stripes though I
cud niver get sight av his face—'who is that
corp'ril man that comes in always whin I'm
goin' away?'

"'Mother av God!' sez she, turnin' as
white as me belt; 'have you seen him, too?'

"'Seen him!' sez I; 'av coorse I have.
Did ye want me not to see him, for'—we
were standin' talkin' in the dhark, outside
the veranda av Bragin's quarters—'you'd
betther tell me to shut me eyes. Onless
I'm mistaken, he's come now.'

"An', sure enough, the corp'ril man was
walkin' to us, hangin' his head down as
though he was ashamed av himsilf.

"'Good-night, Mrs. Bragin,' sez I, very
cool; ''tis not for me to interfere wid your

*a-m001s;* but you might manage these things wid more dacincy. I'm off to canteen,' I sez.

"I turned on my heel an' wint away, swearin' I wud give that man a dhressin' that wud shtop him messin' about the married quarters for a month an' a week. I had not tuk ten paces before Annie Bragin was hangin' on to me arm, an' I cud feel that she was shakin' all over.

"'Stay wid me, Mister Mulvaney,' sez she; 'you're flesh an' blood, at the least— are ye not?'

"'I'm all that,' sez I, an' my anger wint away in a flash. 'Will I want to be asked twice, Annie?'

"Wid that I slipped me arm round her waist, for, begad, I fancied she had surrindered at discretion, an' the honors av war were mine.

"'Fwhat nonsince is this?' sez she, dhrawin' hersilf up on the tips av her dear little toes. 'Wid the mother's milk not dhry on your impident mouth? Let go!' she sez.

"'Did ye not say just now that I was flesh an' blood?' sez I. 'I have not changed since,' I sez; an' I kep' me arm where ut was.

"'Your arms to yoursilf!' sez she, an' her eyes sparkild.

"'Sure, 'tis only human nature,' sez I; an' I kep' me arm where ut was.

"'Nature or no nature,' sez she, 'you take

your arm away or I'll tell Bragin, an' he'll
alter the nature av your head. Fwhat d'you
take me for?' she sez.

"'A woman,' sez I; 'the prettiest in barricks.'

"'A wife,' sez she; 'the straightest in cantonmints!'

"Wid that I dropped me arm, fell back
tu paces, an' saluted, for I saw that she mint
fwhat she said."

"Then you know something that some
men would give a good deal to be certain of.
How could you tell?" I demanded, in the
interests of science.

"Watch the hand," said Mulvaney; "av
she shuts her hand tight, thumb down over
the knuckle, take up your hat an' go. You'll
only make a fool av yoursilf av you shtay.
But av the hand lies opin on the lap, or av
you see her thryin' to shut ut, an' she can't
—go on! She's not past reasonin' wid.

"Well, as I was sayin', I fell back, saluted,
an' was goin' away.

"'Shtay wid me,' she sez. 'Look! He's
comin' again.'

"She pointed to the veranda, an' by the
hoight av impart'nince, the corp'ril man was
comin' out av Bragin's quarters.

"'He's done that these five evenin's past,'
sez Annie Bragin. 'Oh, fwhat will I do?'

"'He'll not do ut again,' sez I, for I was
fightin' mad.

"Kape away from a man that has been a

thrifle crossed in love till the fever's died
down.   He rages like a brute baste.

"I wint up to the man in the veranda,
manin', as sure as I sit, to knock the life out
av him.   He slipped into the open.   'Fwhat
are you doin' philanderin' about here, ye
scum av the gutter?' sez I, polite, to give
him his warnin', for I wanted him ready.

"He niver lifted his head, but sez, all
mournful an' melancolius, as if he thought
I wud be sorry for him : 'I can't find her,'
sez he.

"'My troth,' sez I, 'you've lived too long
—you an' your seekin's an' findin's in a dacint married woman's quarters!   Hould up
your head, ye frozen thief av Genesis,' sez I,
'an' you'll find all you want an' more!'

"But he niver hild up, an' I let go from
the shoulder to where the hair is short over
the eyebrows.

"'That'll do your business,' sez I, but it
nearly did mine instid.   I put me body-
weight behind the blow, but I hit nothin' at
all, an' near put my shoulther out.   The
corp'ril man was not there, an' Annie Bragin, who had been watchin' from the veranda, throws up her heels an' carries on
like a cock whin his neck's wrung by the
dhrummer-bhoy.   I wint back to her, for a
livin' woman, an' a woman like Annie Bragin, is more than a p'rade-groun' full av
ghosts.   I'd never seen a woman faint before, an' I stud it like a shtuck calf, askin'

her whether she was dead, an' prayin' her
for the love av me, an' the love av her husband, an' the love av the Virgin, to open her
blessed eyes again, an' callin' mesilf all the
names undher the canopy av hivin for
plaguin' her wid my miserable *a-moors* whin
I ought to ha' stud betune her an' this corp'ril
man that had lost the number av his mess.

"I misremimber fwhat nonsince I said,
but I was not so far gone that I cud not hear
a fut on the dirt outside. 'Twas Bragin
comin' in, an' by the same token Annie was
comin' to. I jumped to the far end av the
veranda an' looked as if butter wudn't melt
in me mout'. But Mrs. Quinn, the quarter-master's wife that was, had tould Bragin
about me hangin' round Annie.

" 'I'm not pleased wid you, Mulvaney,'
sez Bragin, unbucklin' his sword, for he had
been on duty.

" 'That's bad hearin', I sez, an' I knew
that the pickets were dhriven in. 'What
for, sarjint?' sez I.

" 'Come outside,' sez he, 'an' I'll show
you why.'

" 'I'm willin,' I sez; 'but me stripes are
none so ould that I can afford to lose thim.
Tell me now, who do I go out wid?' sez I.

"He was a quick man an' a just man, an'
saw fwhat I wud be afther. 'Wid Mrs.
Bragin's husband,' sez he. He might ha'
known by me askin' that favor that I had
done him no wrong.

**6**

"We wint to the back av the arsenal an' I stripped to him, an' for ten minutes 'twas all I could do to prevint him killin' himself against me fistes. He was mad as a dumb dog—just frothing with rage; but he had no chanst wid me in reach, or learnin', or anything else.

"'Will ye hear reason?' sez I, when his first wind was runnin' out.

"'Not whoile I can see,' sez he. Wid that I gave him both, one after the other, smash through the low gyard that he'd been taught whin he was a boy, an' the eyebrow shut down on the cheek-bone like the wing of a sick crow.

"'Will ye hear reason now, ye brave man?' sez I.

"'Not whoile I can speak,' sez he, staggerin' up blind as a stump. I was loath to do ut, but I wint round an' swung into the jaw side-on an' shifted ut a half pace to the lef'.

"'Will you hear reason now?' sez I; 'I can't keep my timper much longer, an' 'tis like I will hurt you.'

"'Not whoile I can stand,' he mumbles out av one corner av his mouth. So I closed an' threw him—blind, dumb, an' sick, an' jammed the jaw straight.

"'You're an ould fool, Mister Bragin,' sez I.

"'You're a young thief,' sez he, 'an' you've bruk me heart, you an' Annie betune you!'

"Thin he began cryin' like a child as he

lay. I was sorry as I had niver been before.
'Tis an awful thing to see a strong man cry.

" ' I'll swear on the cross,' sez I.

" ' I care for none av your oaths,' sez he.

" ' Come back to your quarters,' sez I, ' an
if you don't believe the livin', begad, you
shall listen to the dead,' I sez.

" I hoisted him an' tuk him back to his
quarters. 'Mrs. Bragin,' sez I, ' here's a man
you can cure quicker than me.'

" ' You've shamed me before me wife,' he
whimpers.

" ' Have I so ?' sez I. 'By the look on
Mrs. Bragin's face I think I'm in for a
dhressin'-down worse than I gave you.'

" An' I was! Annie Bragin was woild
wid indignation. There was not a name
that a dacint woman cud use that was not
given my way. I've had me colonel walk
roun' me like a cooper roun' a cask for fifteen minutes in ord'ly room bekaze I wint
into the corner shop an unstrapped lewnatic,
but all that I iver tuk from his rasp av a
tongue was ginger-pop to fwhat Annie tould
me. An' that, mark you, is the way av a
woman.

" Whin ut was done for want av breath,
an' Annie was bendin' over her husband, I
sez : ' 'Tis all thrue, an' I'm a blayguard an'
you're an honest woman ; but will you tell
him of wan service that I did you ?'

" As I finished speakin' the corp'ril came
**up to the veranda, an' Annie Bragin**

shqualed. The moon was up, an' we cud
see his face.

"'I can't find her,' sez the corp'ril man,
an' wint out like the puff av a candle.

"'Saints stand betune us an' evil!' sez
Bragin, crossin' himself; 'that's Flahy av
the Tyrone Rig'mint.'

"'Who was he?' I sez, 'for he has given
me a dale av fightin' this day.'

"Bragin tould us that Flahy was a cor-
p'ril who lost his wife av cholera in those
quarters three years gone, an' wint mad, an'
'walked' afther they buried him, huntin' for
her.

"'Well,' sez I to Bragin, 'he's been
hookin' out av purgathory to kape company
wid Mrs. Bragin ivry evenin' for the last
fortnight. You may tell Mrs. Quinn, wid
my love, for I know that she's been talkin'
to you, an' you've been listenin', that she
ought to ondherstand the differ 'twixt a man
an' a ghost. She's had three husbands,' sez
I, 'an' you've got a wife too good for you.
Instid av which you lave her to be boddered
by ghosts an'—an' all manner av evil spir-
ruts. I'll niver go talkin' in the way av politeness to a man's wife again. Good-night
to you both,' sez I, an' wid that I wint away,
havin' fought wid woman, man an' divil all
in the heart av an hour. By the same token
I gave Father Victor wan rupee to say mass
for Flahy's soul, me havin' discommoded
him by shtickin' my fist into his systim."

"Your ideas of politeness seem rather large, Mulvaney," I said.

"That's as you look at ut," said Mulvaney, calmly; "Annie Bragin niver cared for me. For all that, I did not want to leave anything behin' me that Bragin could take hould av to be angry wid her about, whin an honust wurrud cud ha' cleared all up. There's nothin' like opin-speakin'. Orth'ris, ye scut, let me put me oi to that bottle, for me throat's as dhry as whin I thought I wud get a kiss from Annie Bragin. An' that's fourteen years gone! Eyah! Cork's own city an' the blue sky above ut—an' the times that was—the times that was!"

# WITH THE MAIN GUARD.

Der jungere Uhlanen
Sit round mit open mouth
While Breitmann tell dem stdories
Of fightin' in the South ;
Und gif dem moral lessons,
How before der battle pops,
Take a little prayer to Himmel
Und a goot long drink of Schnapps.
*Hans Breitmann's Ballads.*

"Mary, Mother av Mercy, fwhat the divil possist us to take an' kape this melancolius counthry?   Answer me that, sorr."

It was Mulvaney who was speaking. The hour was one o'clock of a stifling hot June night, and the place was the main gate of Fort Amara, most desolate and least desirable of all the fortresses in India. What I was doing there at that hour is a question which only concerns McGrath, the sergeant of the guard, and the men on the gate.

"Slape," said Mulvaney, "is a shuparfluous necessity. This gyard'll shtay till relieved." He himself was stripped to the waist; Learoyd on the next bedstead was dripping from the skinful of water which Ortheris, arrayed only in white trousers, had just sluiced over his shoulders; and a fourth

( 86 )

private was muttering uneasily as he dozed open-mouthed in the glare of the great guard-lantern. The heat under the bricked archway was terrifying.

"The worrst night that iver I remimber. Eyah! Is all hell loose this tide?" said Mulvaney. A puff of burning wind lashed through the wicket-gate like a wave of the sea, and Ortheris swore.

"Are ye more heasy, Jock?" he said to Learoyd. "Put yer 'ead between yer legs. It'll go orf in a minute."

"Ah don't care. Ah would not care, but ma heart is plaayin' tivvy-tivvy on ma ribs. Let me die! Oh, leave me die!" groaned the huge Yorkshire man, who was feeling the heat acutely, being of fleshly build.

The sleeper under the lantern roused for a moment and raised himself on his elbow, "Die and be damned, then!" he said. "I'm damned and I can't die!"

"Who's that?" I whispered, for the voice was new to me.

"Gentleman born," said Mulvaney. "Corp'ril wan year, sarjint nex'. Red-hot on his c'mission, but dhrinks like a fish. He'll be gone before the cowld weather's here. So!"

He slipped his boot, and with the naked toe just touched the trigger of his Martini. Ortheris misunderstood the movement, and the next instant the Irishman's rifle was dashed aside, while Ortheris stood before him, his eyes blazing with reproof.

"You!" said Ortheris. "My Gawd, you! If it was you, wot would we do?"

"Kape quiet, little man," said Mulvaney, putting him aside, but very gently; "'tis not me, nor will ut be me whoile Dinah Shadd's here. I was but showin' somethin'."

Learoyd, bowed on his bedstead, groaned, and the gentleman ranker sighed in his sleep. Ortheris took Mulvaney's tendered pouch, and we three smoked gravely for a space while the dust-devils danced on the glacis and scoured the red-hot plain without.

"Pop?" said Ortheris, wiping his forehead.

"Don't tantalize wid talkin' av dhrink, or I'll shtuff you into your own breech-block an' fire you off!" grunted Mulvaney.

Ortheris chuckled, and from a niche in the veranda produced six bottles of gingerade.

"Where did ye get ut, ye Machiavel?" said Mulvaney. "'Tis no bazaar pop."

"'Ow do Hi know wot the orf'cers drink?" answered Ortheris. "Arst the mess-man."

"Ye'll have a disthrict coort-martial settin' on ye yet, me son," said Mulvaney, "but" —he opened a bottle—"I will not report ye this time. Fwhat's in the mess-kid is mint for the belly, as they say, 'specially whin that mate is dhrink. Here's luck! A bloody war or a—no, we've got the sickly season. War, thin!"—he waved the innocent "pop" to the four quarters of heaven. "Bloody war! north, east, south an' west! Jock, ye quakin' hayrick, come an' dhrink."

But Learoyd, half mad with the fear of death presaged in the swelling veins of his neck, was imploring his Maker to strike him dead, and fighting for more air between his prayers. A second time Ortheris drenched the quivering body with water, and the giant revived.

" An' Ah divn't see thot a mon is i' fettle for gooin' on to live; an' Ah divn't see thot there is owt for t' livin' for. Hear now, lads! Ah'm tired—tired. There's nobbut water i' ma bones. Let me die!"

The hollow of the arch gave back Learoyd's broken whisper in a bass boom. Mulvaney looked at me hopelessly, but I remembered how the madness of despair had once fallen upon Ortheris, that weary, weary afternoon on the banks of the Khemi River, and how it had been exorcised by the skillful magician Mulvaney.

"Talk, Terence!" I said, "or we shall have Learoyd slinging loose, and he'll be worse than Ortheris was. Talk! He'll answer to your voice."

Almost before Ortheris had deftly thrown all the rifles of the guard on Mulvaney's bedstead, the Irishman's voice was uplifted as that of one in the middle of a story, and, turning to me, he said:

"In barricks or out of it, as you say, sorr, an Oirish rig'mint is the divil an' more. 'Tis only fit for a young man wid eddicated fisteses. Oh, the crame av disruption is an Oirish rig'mint, an' rippin', tearin', ragin' scattherers in the field av war! My first rig'mint was Oirish—Faynians an' rebils to the heart av their marrow was they, an' so they fought for the widdy betther than most, bein' contrairy—Oirish. They was the Black Tyrone. You've heard av thim, sorr?"

Heard of them! I knew the Black Tyrone for the choicest collection of unmitigated blackguards, dog-stealers, robbers of hen-roosts, assaulters of innocent citizens, and recklessly daring heroes in the Army List. Half Europe and half Asia has had cause to know the Black Tyrone—good luck be to their tattered colors as glory has ever been!

"They was hot pickils and ginger! I cut a man's head tu deep wid my belt in the days av my youth, an', afther some circumstances which I will oblitherate, I came to the ould rig'mint, bearin' the character av a man wid hands an' feet. But, as I was goin' to tell you, I fell acrost the Black Tyrone ag'in wan day whin we wanted thim powerful bad. Orth'ris, me son, fwhat was the name av that place where they sint wan comp'ny av us an' wan av the Tyrone roun' a hill an' down again, all for to tache the Paythans somethin' they'd niver learned before? Afther Ghuzni 'twas."

"Don't know what the bloomin' Paythans

called it. We called it Silver's Theayter. You know that, sure!"

"Silver's Theatre—so 'twas. A gut betune two hills, as black as a bucket, an' as thin as a gurl's waist. There was overmany Paythans for our convaynience in the gut, an' begad they called thimsilves a reserve—bein' impident by natur! Our Scotchies an' lashins av Gurkys was poundin' into some Paythan rig'mints, I think 'twas. Scotchies an' 'Gurkys are twins bekaze they're so onlike, an' they get dhrunk together whin God plases. Well, as I was sayin', they sint wan comp'ny av the Ould an' wan av the Tyrone to double up the hill an' clane out the Paythan reserve. Orf'cers was scarce in thim days, fwhat wid dysintry an' not takin' care av thimselves, an' we was sint out wid only wan orf'cer for the comp'ny; but he was a man that had his feet beneath him, an' all his teeth in their sockuts."

"Who was he?" I asked.

"Captain O'Neil—Old Crook—Cruik-na-bulleen—him that I tould ye that tale av whin he was in Burmah. Hah! He was a man. The Tyrone tuk a little orf'cer bhoy, but divil a bit was he in command, as I'll dimonstrate presintly. We an' they came over the brow av the hill, wan on each side av the gut, an' there was that ondacint reserve waitin' down below like rats in a pit.

"'Howld on, men,' sez Crook, who tuk a

mother's care av us always. 'Rowl some
rocks on thim by way av visitin'-kyards.'
We hadn't rowled more than twinty bowl-
ders, an' the Paythans was beginnin' to
swear tremenjus, whin the little orf-cer bhoy
av the Tyrone shqueaks out acrost the valley: 'Fwhat the divil an' all are you doin',
shpoilin' the fun for my men? Do ye not
see they'll stand?"

"'Faith, that's a rare pluckt wan!' sez
Crook. 'Niver mind the rocks, men. Come
along down an' take tay wid thim!'

"'There's damned little sugar in ut!' sez
my rear-rank man; but Crook heard.

"'Have ye not all got spoons?' he sez,
laughin', an' down we wint as fast as we cud.
Learoyd bein' sick at the base, he, av coorse,
was not there."

"Thot's a lie!" said Learoyd, dragging his
bedstead nearer. " Ah gotten *thot* theer, an'
you knaw it, Mulvaney." He threw up his
arms, and from the right arm-pit ran, diago-
nally through the fell of his chest, a thin
white line terminating near the fourth left
rib.

"My mind's goin'," said Mulvaney, the
unabashed. " Ye were there. Fwhat was
I thinkin' of? 'Twas another man, av
coorse. Well, you'll remimber thin, Jock,
how we an' the Tyrone met wid a bang at
the bottom an' got jammed past all movin'
among the Paythans."

"Ow! It was a tight 'ole. Hi was squeeged

till I thought I'd bloomin' well bust," said Ortheris, rubbing his stomach meditatively.

" 'Twas no place for a little man, but wan little man"—Mulvaney put his hand on Ortheris's shoulder—" saved the life av me. There we shtuck, for divil a bit did the Paythans flinch, an' divil a bit dare we; our business bein' to clear 'em out. An' the most exthryordinar' thing av all was that we an' they just rushed into each other's arrums, an' there was no firin' for a long time. Nothin' but knife an' bay'nit when we cud get our hands free; that was not often. We was breast on to thim, an' the Tyrone was yelpin' behind av us in a way I didn't see the lean av at first. But I knew later, an' so did the Paythans.

" 'Knee to knee!' sings out Crook, wid a laugh whin the rush av our comin' into the gut shtopped, an' he was huggin' a hairy Paythan, neither bein' able to do anything to the other, tho' both was wishful.

" ' Breast to breast!' he says, as the Tyrone was pushin' us forward closer an' closer.

" ' An' han' over back !' sez a sarjint that was behin'. I saw a sword lick out past Crook's ear like a snake's tongue, an' the Paythan was tuk in the apple av his throat like a pig at Dromeen fair.

" 'Thank ye, Brother Inner Guard,' sez Crook, cool as a cucumber widout salt. 'I wanted that room.' An' he wint forward by the thickness av a man's body, havin' turned the Paythan undher him. The man bit the heel off Crook's boot in his death-bite.

"'Push, men!' sez Crook. 'Push, ye paper-backed beggars!' he sez. 'Am I to pull ye through?' So we pushed, an' we kicked, an' we swung, an' we swore, an' the grass bein' slippery, our heels wouldn't bite, an' God help the front-rank man that wint down that day!"

"'Ave you ever bin in the pit hentrance o' the Vic. on a thick night?" interrupted Ortheris. "It was worse nor that, for they was goin' one way, an' we wouldn't 'ave it. Leastaways, Hi 'adn't much to say."

"Faith, me son, ye said ut, thin. I kep' the little man betune my knees as long as I cud, but he was pokin' roun' wid his bay'-nit, blindin' an' stiffin' feroshus. The divil of a man is Orth'ris in a ruction—aren't ye?" said Mulvaney.

"Don't make game!" said the cockney. "I knowed I wasn't no good then, but I guv 'em compot from the lef' flank when we opened out. No!" he said, bringing down his hand with a thump on the bedstead, "a bay'nit ain't no good to a little man—might as well 'ave a bloomin' fishin'-rod! I 'ate a clawin', maulin' mess, but gimme a breech that's wore out a bit, an' hamminition one year in store, to let the powder kiss the bul-let, an' put me somewheres where I ain't trod on by 'ulkin swine like you, an' s'elp

me Gawd, I could bowl you over five times
outer seven at height 'undred. Would yer
try, you lumberin' Hirishman?"

"No, ye wasp. I've seen ye do ut. I say
there's nothin' better than the bay'nit, wid
a long reach, a double twist av ye can, an' a
slow recover."

"Dom the bay'nit," said Learoyd, who
had been listening intently. "Look a-here!"
He picked up a rifle an inch below the
foresight with an underhanded action, and
used it exactly as a man would use a dagger.

"Sitha," said he, softly, "thot's better
than owt, for a mon can bash t' faace wi' thot,
an', if he divn't, he can breeak t' forearm o' t'
gaard. 'Tis not i' t' books, though. Give
me t' butt."

"Each does ut his own way, like makin'
love," said Mulvaney, quietly; "the butt or
the bay'nit or the bullet accordin' to the
natur' av the man. Well, as I was sayin',
we shtuck there breathin' in each other's
faces an' swearin' powerful, Orth'ris cursin'
the mother that bore him bekaze he was not
three inches taller.

"Prisintly he sez: 'Duck, ye lump, an' I
can get at a man over your shouldher!'"

"'You'll blow me head off,' I sez, throwin'
me arm clear; 'go through under me arm-
pit, ye blood-thirsty little scut,' sez I, 'but
don't shtick me or I'll wring your ears
round.'

"Fwhat was ut ye gave the Paythan man

forninst me, him that cut at me whin I cudn't move hand or foot? Hot or cowld was ut?"

"Cold," said Ortheris, "up an' under the rib-jint. 'E come down flat. Best for you 'e did."

"Thrue, me son! This jam thing that I'm talkin' about lasted for five minutes good, an' thin we got our arms clear an' wint in. I misremimber exactly fwhat I did, but I didn't want Dinah to be a widdy at the Depot. Thin, after some promishku-ous hackin' we shtuck again, an' the Tyrone behin' was callin' us dogs an' cowards an' all manner av names; we barrin' their way.

"'Fwhat ails the Tyrone?' thinks I; 'they've the makin's av a most convanient fight here.'

"'A man behind me sez beseechful an' in a whisper: 'Let me get at thim! For the love of Mary give me room beside ye, ye tall man!'

"'An' who are you that's so anxious to be kilt?' sez I, widout turnin' my head, for the long knives was dancin' in front like the sun on Donegal Bay whin ut's rough.

"'We've seen our dead,' he sez, squeezin' into me; 'our dead that was men two days gone! An' me that was his cousin by blood could not bring Tim Coulan off! Let me get on,' he sez, 'let me get to thim or I'll run ye through the back!'

"'My troth,' thinks I, 'if the Tyrone have

seen their dead, God help the Paythans this day !'  An' thin I knew why the Oirish was ragin' behind us as they was.

"I gave room to the man, an' he ran forward wid the Haymakers' Lift on his bay'nit an' swung a Paythan clear off his feet by the belly-band av the brute, an' the iron bruk at the lockin'-ring.

"'Tim Coulan 'll slape aisy to-night,' sez he wid a grin; an' the next minut his head was in two halves an' he wint down grinnin' by sections.

"The Tyrone was pushin' an' pushin' in, an' our men was swearin' at thim, an' Crook was workin' away in front av us, his sword-arm swingin' like a pump-handle an' his revolver spittin' like a cat.  But the strange thing av ut was the quiet that lay upon. 'Twas like a fight in a drame—except for thim that was dead.

"Whin I gave room to the Oirishman I was expinded an' forlorn in my inside. 'Tis a way I have, savin' your prisince, sorr, in acticn.  'Let me out, bhoys,' sez I, backin' in among thim.  'I'm goin' to be onwell!' Faith they gave me room at the wurrud, though they would not ha' given room for all hell wid the chill off.  Whin I got clear, I was, savin' your prisince, sorr, outragis sick bekaze I had dhrunk heavy that day.

"Well an' far out av harm was a sarjint av the Tyrone sittin' on the little orf'cer bhoy who had stopped Crook from rowlin'
7

the rocks.   Oh, he was a beautiful bhoy, an'
the long black curses was slidin' out av his
innocint mouth like mornin'-jew from a
rose!

"' Fwhat have you got there?' sez I to the
sarjint.

"' Wan av her majesty's bantams wid his
spurs up,' sez he.   ' He's goin' to coort-martial me.'

"' Let me go !' sez the little orf'cer bhoy.
' Let me go an' command me men !' mainin'
thereby the Black Tyrone, which was beyond
any command—ay, even av they had made
the divil a field-orf'cer.

"' His father howlds me mother's cow-
feed in Clonmel,' sez the man that was sittin' on him.   ' Will I go back to his mother
an' tell her that I've let him throw himself
away ?   Lie still, ye little pinch of dyna-
mite, an' coort-martial me afterwards.'

"' Good,' sez I; ' 'tis the likes av him
makes the likes av the commandher-in chief,
but we must presarve thim.   Fwhat d' you
want to do, sorr ?' sez I, very politeful.

"' Kill the beggars—kill the beggars !' he
shqueaks, his blue eyes fairly brimmin' wid
tears.

"' An' how'll ye do that ?' sez I.   ' You've
shquibbed off your revolver like a child wid
a cracker; you can make no play wid that
fine large  sword av yours; an' your hand's
shakin' like an asp on a leaf.   Lie still and
grow,' sez I.

"'Get back to your comp'ny,' sez he; 'you're insolint!'

"'All in good time,' sez I; 'but I'll have a dhrink first."

"Just thin Crook comes up, blue an' white all over where he wasn't red.

"'Wather!' sez he; 'I'm dead wid drouth! Oh, but it's a gran' day!'

"He dhrank half a skinful, and the rest he tilts into his chest, an' it fair hissed on the hairy hide av him. He sees the little orf'cer bhoy undher the sarjint.

"'Fwat's yonder?' sez he.

"'Mutiny, sorr,' sez the sarjint, an' the orf'cer bhoy begins pleadin' pitiful to Crook to be let go; but divil a bit wud Crook budge.

"'Kape him there,' he sez; ''tis no child's work this day. By the same token,' sez he, 'I'll confishcate that iligant nickel-plated scent-sprinkler av yours, for me own has been vomitin' dishgraceful!'

"The fork av his hand was black wid the back-spit of the machine. So he tuk the orf'cer bhoy's revolver. Ye may look, sorr, but, by me faith, there's a dale more done in the field than iver gets into field ordhers!

"'Come on, Mulvaney,' sez Crook; 'is this a coort-martial?' The two av us wint back together into the mess an' the Paythans were still standin' up. They was not too impart'nint though, for the Tyrone was callin' wan to another to remimber Tim Coulan.

" Crook stopped outside av the strife an' looked anxious, his eyes rollin' roun'.

" ' Fwhat is ut, sorr ?' sez I; ' can I get ye anything ?'

" ' Where's a bugler ?' sez he.

" I wint into the crowd—our men was dhrawin' breath behin' the Tyrone who was fightin' like sowls in tormint—an' prisintly I came acrost little Frehan, our bugler bhoy, pokin' roun' among the best wid a rifle an' bay'nit.

" ' Is amusin' yoursilf fwhat you're paid for, ye limb ?' sez I, catchin' him by the scruff. ' Come out av that an' attind to your duty,' I sez; but the bhoy was not pleased.

" ' I've got wan,' sez he, grinnin', ' big as you, Mulvaney, an' fair half as ugly. Let me go get another.'

" I was dishpleased at the personability av that remark, so I tucks him under me arm an' carries him to Crook, who was watchin' how the fight wint. Crook cuffs him till the bhoy cries, an' thin sez nothin' for a whoile.

" The Paythans began to flicker onaisy, an' our men roared. ' Opin ordher! Double !' sez Crook. ' Blow, child, blow for the honor av the British arrmy !'

" That bhoy blew like a typhoon, an' the Tyrone an' we opined out as the Paythans broke, an' I saw that fwhat had gone before wud be kissin' an' huggin' to fwhat was to come. We'd dhruv thim into a broad part av the gut whin they gave, and thin we opined out an' fair danced down the valley, dhrivin' thim before us. Oh, 'twas lovely, an' stiddy, too! There was the sarjints on the flanks av what was left av us, kapin' touch, an' the fire was runnin' from flank to flank, an' the Paythans was dhroppin'. We opined out wid the widenin' av the valley, an' whin the valley narrowed we closed again like the shticks on a lady's fan, an' at the far ind av the gut where they thried to stand we fair blew them off their feet, for we had expinded very little ammunition by reason av the knife work."

"Hi used thirty rounds goin' down that valley," said Ortheris, "an' it was gentle-man's work. Might 'a' done it in a white 'andkerchief an' pink silk stockin's, that part. Hi was on in that piece."

"You could ha' heard the Tyrone yellin' a mile away," said Mulvaney, "an' 'twas all their sarjints cud do to get thim off. They was mad—mad—mad! Crook sits down in the quiet that fell whin we had gone down the valley, an' covers his face wid his hands. Prisintly we all came back accordin' to our natures and disposisihins, for they, mark you, show through the hide av a man in that hour.

"'Bhoys! bhoys!' sez Crook to himself. 'I misdoubt we could ha' engaged at long range an' saved betther men than me.' He looked at our dead an' said no more.

" ' Captain dear,' sez a man av the Tyrone
comin' up wid his mouth bigger than iver
his mother kissed ut, spittin' blood like a
whale; ' captain,' sez he, ' if wan or two in
the sthalls have been discommoded, the gallery have enjoyed the performinces av a
Roshus.'

" Thin I knew that man for the Dublin
dock-rat he was—wan of the bhoys that
made the lessee av Silver's Theatre gray before his time wid tearin' out the bowils av
the benches an' t'rowin' thim into the pit.
So I passed the wurrud that I knew when I
was in the Tyrone an' we lay in Dublin. ' I
don't know who 'twas,' I whispers, ' an' I
don't care, but any ways I'll knock the face
av you, Tim Kelley."

"' Eyah!' sez the man, ' was you thère,
too? We'll call ut Silver's Theatre.' Half
the Tyrone, knowin' the ould place, tuk ut
up; so we called it Silver's Theatre.

" The little orf'cer bhoy av the Tyrone
was thrimblin' an' cryin'. He had no heart
for the coort-martials that he talked so big
upon. ' Ye'll do well later,' sez Crook, very
quiet, ' for not bein' allowed to kill yourself for amusemint.'

"' I'm a dishgraced man!' sez the little
orf'cer bhoy.

"' Put me undher arrest, sorr, if you will,
but, by me sowl, I'd do ut again sooner than
face your mother wid you dead,' sez the sarjint that had sat on his head, standin' to

attention an' salutin'. But the young wan only cried as tho' his little heart was breakin'.

"Thin another man av the Tyrone came up, wid the fog av fightin' on him."

"The what, Mulvaney?"

"Fog av fightin'. You know, sorr, that, like makin luv, ut takes each man dif'rint. Now, I can't help bein' powerful sick whin I'm in action. Orth'ris, here, niver stops swearin' from ind to ind, an' the only time that Learoyd opins his mouth to sing is whin he is messin' wid other people's heads; for he's a dhirty fighter is Jock Learoyd. Recruities sometime cry, an' sometime they don't know fwhat they do, an' sometime they are all for cuttin' throats, an' such like dirtiness; but some men get heavy-head-dhrunk on the fightin'. This man was. He was staggerin', an' his eyes were half shut' an' we cud hear him dhraw breath twinty yards away. He sees the little orf'cer bhoy, an' comes up, talkin' thick an' drowsy to himsilf. 'Blood the young whelp!' he sez; 'blood the young whelp;' an' wid that he threw up his arms, shpun roun', an' dropped at our feet, dead as a Paythan, an' there was niver sign or scratch on him. They said 'twas his heart was rotten, but oh, 'twas a quare thing to see!

"Thin we wint to bury our dead, for we wud not lave them to the Paythans, an' in

movin' among the haythen we nearly lost
that little orf'cer bhoy.  He was for givin'
wan divil wather and layin' him aisy against
a rock.  'Be careful, sorr,' sez I; 'a wounded
Paythan's worse than a live wan.'  My
troth, before the words was out of me mouth,
the man on the ground fires at the orf'cer
bhoy lanin' over him, an' I saw the helmit
fly.  I dropped the butt on the face av the
man an' tuk his pistol.  The little orf'cer
bhoy turned very white, for the hair av half
his head was singed away.

"'I tould you so, sorr!' sez I; an' afther
that, whin he wanted to help a Paythan I
stud wid the muzzle contagious to the ear.
They dare not do anythin' but curse.  The
Tyrone was growlin' like dogs over a bone
that had been taken away too soon, for they
had seen their dead an' they wanted to kill
ivry sowl on the ground.  Crook tould thim
that he'd blow the hide off any man that
misconducted himself; but, seeing that ut
was the first time the Tyrone had iver seen
their dead, I do not wondher they were on
the sharp.  'Tis a shameful sight!  Whin I
first saw ut I wud niver ha' given quarter to
any man north of the Khaibar—no, nor
woman either, for the women used to come
out afther dhark—*Auggrh !*

"Well, evenshually we buried our dead
an' tuk away our wounded, an' come over
the brow av the hills to see the Scotchies an'
the Gurkys taking tay wid the Paythans in

bucketsfuls. We were a gang av dissolute ruffians, for the blood had caked the dust, an' the sweat had cut the cake, an' our bay'-nits was hangin' like butcher's steels betune our legs, an' most av us were marked one way or another.

" A staff orf'cer man, clean as a new rifle, rides up an' sez: ' What damned scarecrows are you ?'

" ' A company av her majesty's Black Ty-rone, an' wan av the ould rig'mint,' sez Crook very quiet, givin' our visitor the flure as 'twas.

" ' Oh !' sez the staff orf'cer, ' did you dis-lodge that reserve ?'

" ' No !' sez Crook, an' the Tyrone laughed.

" ' Thin fwhat the divil have ye done ?'

" ' Disthroyed ut,' sez Crook, an' he took us on, but not before Toomey that was in the Tyrone sez aloud, his voice somewhere in his stummick : ' Fwhat in the name av mis-fortune does this parrit widout a tail mane by shtoppin' the road av his betthers ?'

" The staff orf'cer wint blue, and Toomey makes him pink by changin' to the voice av a minowderin' woman an' sayin': 'Come an' kiss me, major dear, for me husband's at the wars, an' I'm all alone at the depot.'

" The staff orf'cer wint away, an' I cud see Crook's shoulthers shakin'.

" His corp'ril checks Toomey. 'Lave me alone,' sez Toomey, widout a wink. "I was his bâtman before he was married an' he knows fwhat I mane, av you don't. There's nothin' like livin' in the hoight av society. D'you remimber that, Orth'ris?'

"'Hi do, Toomey; 'e died in 'orspital, next week it was, 'cause I bought 'arf his kit; an' I remember after that—'"

"GUARD, TURN OUT!"

The relief had come; it was four o'clock. "I'll catch a kyart for you, sorr," said Mulvaney, diving hastily into his accouterments. "Come up to the top av the fort an' we'll pershue our invistigations into McGrath's shtable." The relieved guard strolled round the main bastion on its way to the swimming-bath, and Learoyd grew almost talkative. Ortheris looked into the fort ditch and across the plain. "Ho! it's weary waitin' for Ma-ary!" he hummed; "but I'd like to kill some more bloomin' Paythans before my time's up. War! Bloody war! North, east, south and west."

"Amen," said Learoyd, slowly.

"Fwhat's here?" said Mulvaney, checking at a blur of white by the foot of the old sentry box. He stooped and touched it. "It's Norah—Norah McTaggart! Why, Nonie darlin', fwhat are ye doin' out av your mother's bed at this time?"

The two-year-old child of Sergeant McTaggart must have wandered for a breath of cool air to the very verge of the parapet of the fort ditch. Her tiny night-shift was gathered into a wisp round her neck and she

moaned in her sleep. "See there!" said
Mulvaney; "poor lamb! Look at the heat-
rash on the innocent skin av her. 'Tis hard
—crool hard even for us. Fwhat must it be
for these? Wake up, Nonie, your mother
will be woild about you. Begad, the child
might ha' fallen into the ditch!"

He picked her up in the growing light,
and set her on his shoulder, and her fair
curls touched the grizzled stubble of his
temples. Ortheris and Learoyd followed,
snapping their fingers, while Norah smiled
at them a sleepy smile. Then caroled Mulvaney, clear as a lark, dancing the baby on
his arm:

> "If any young man should marry you,
>    Say nothin' about the joke;
>  That iver ye slep' in a sinthry box,
>    Wrapped up in a soldier's cloak."

"Though, on me sowl, Nonie," he said,
gravely, "there was not much cloak about
you. Niver mind, you won't dhress like
this ten years to come. Kiss your friends
an' run along to your mother."

Nonie, set down close to the married
quarters, nodded with the quiet obedience
of the soldier's child, but, ere she pattered
off over the flagged path, held up her lips to
be kissed by the three musketeers. Ortheris
wiped his mouth with the back of his hand
and swore sentimentally; Learoyd turned
pink; and the two walked away together.

The Yorkshireman lifted up his voice and gave in thunder the chorus of " The Sentry Box," while Ortheris piped at his side.

" 'Bin to a bloomin' sing-song, you two ?" said the artilleryman, who was taking his cartridge down to the Morning Gun. " You're overmerry for these dashed days."

> " I bid ye take care o' the brat, said he,
>     For it comes of a noble race,"

bellowed Learoyd. The voices died out in the swimming-bath.

" Oh, Terence !" I said, dropping into Mulvaney's speech, when we were alone, " it's you that have the tongue !"

He looked at me wearily ; his eyes were sunk in his head, and his face was drawn and white. " Eyah !" said he ; " I've blandandhered thim through the night somehow, but can thim that helps others help thimselves? Answer me that, sorr !"

And over the bastions of Fort Amara broke the pitiless day.

# BLACK JACK.

To the wake av Tim O'Hara
 Came company,
All St. Patrick's Alley
 Was there to see.
*The Wake of Tim O'Hara.*

THERE is a writer called Mr. Robert Louis
Stevenson, who makes most delicate inlay-
work in black and white, and files out to
the fraction of a hair. He has written a
story about a suicide club, wherein men
gambled for death, because other amuse-
ments did not bite sufficiently. My friend
Private Mulvaney knows nothing about Mr.
Stevenson, but he once assisted informally
at a meeting of almost such a club as that
gentleman has described ; and his words are
true.

As the Three Musketeers share their silver,
tobacco, and liquor together, as they protect
each other in barracks or camp, and as they
rejoice together over the joy of one, so do
they divide their sorrows. When Ortheris's
irrepressible tongue has brought him into
cells for a season, or Learoyd has run amuck
through his kit and accouterments, or Mulvaney has indulged in strong waters, and
under their influence reproved his com-

(109)

manding officer, you can see the trouble in
the faces of the untouched twain.  And the
rest of the regiment know that comment or
jest is unsafe.  Generally the three avoid
orderly-room and the corner shop that fol-
lows, leaving both to the young bloods who
have not sown their wild oats; but there are
occasions . . .  For instance, Ortheris was
sitting on the new draw-bridge of the main
gate of Fort Amara, with his hands in his
pockets and his pipe, bowl down, in his
mouth.  Learoyd was lying at full length
on the turf of the glacis, kicking his heels
in the air, and I came round the corner and
asked for Mulvaney.

Ortheris spat into the ditch and shook his
head.  "No good seein' 'im now," said Ortheris; 'e's a bloomin' camel.  Listen."

I heard on the flags of the veranda oppo-
site to the cells, which are close to the guard-
room, a measured step that I could have
identified in the tramp of an army.  There
were twenty paces *crescendo*, a pause, and
then twenty *diminuendo*.

"That's 'im," said Ortheris; "my Gawd,
that's 'im!  All for a bloomin' button you
could see your face in an' a bit o' lip that a
bloomin' harkangel would 'a' guv back.''

Mulvaney was doing pack-drill—was com-
pelled, that is to say, to walk up and down
for certain hours in full marching order,
with rifle, bayonet, ammunition, knapsack,
and overcoat.  And his offense was being

dirty on parade! I nearly fell into the fort ditch with astonishment and wrath, for Mulvaney is the smartest man that ever mounted guard, and would as soon think of turning out uncleanly as of dispensing with his trousers.

"Who was the sergeant that checked him?" I asked.

"Mullins, o' course," said Ortheris. "There ain't no other man would whip 'im on the peg so. But Mullins ain't a man. 'E's a dirty little pig-scraper, that's wot 'e is."

"What did Mulvaney say? He's not the make of man to take that quietly."

"Said! Bin better for 'im if 'e'd shut 'is mouth. Lord, 'ow we laughed! 'Sarjint,' 'e sez, 'ye say I'm dirty. Well,' sez 'e, 'when your wife lets you blow your own nose for yourself, perhaps you'll know what dirt is. You're himperfectly eddicated, sarjint,' sez 'e, an' then we fell in. But after p'rade, 'e was up an' Mullins was swearin' 'imself black in the face at ord'ly-room that Mulvaney 'ad called 'im a swine an' Lord knows wot all. You know Mullins. 'E'll 'ave 'is 'ead broke in one o' these days. E's too big a bloomin' liar for ord'nary consumption. 'Three hours' can an' kit,' sez the colonel; 'not for bein' dirty on p'rade, but for 'avin' said somethin' to Mullins, tho' I do not believe,' sez 'e, 'you said wot 'e said you said.' An' Mulvaney fell away sayin' nothin'. You know 'e never speaks to the colonel for fear o' gettin' 'imself fresh copped."

Mullins, a very young and very much married sergeant, whose manners were partly the result of innate depravity and partly of imperfectly digested board school, came over the bridge, and most rudely asked Ortheris what he was doing.

"Me?" said Ortheris. "Ow! I'm waitin' for my c'mission. 'Seed it comin' along yit?"

Mullins turned purple and passed on. There was the sound of a gentle chuckle from the glacis where Learoyd lay.

"'E expects to get his c'mission some day," explained Ortheris; "Gawd 'elp the mess that 'ave to put their 'ands into the same kiddy as 'im! Wot time d'you make it, sir? Fower! Mulvaney 'll be out in 'arf an hour. You don't want to buy a dorg, sir, do you? A pup you can trust—'arf Rampore by the colonel's grey'ound."

" Ortheris," I answered, sternly, for I knew what was in his mind, " do you mean to say that—"

"I didn't mean to arx money o' you, any'ow," said Ortheris; "I'd 'a' sold you the dorg good an' cheap, but—but—I know Mulvaney 'll want somethin' after we've walked 'im orf, an' I ain't got nothin', nor 'e 'asn't neither. I'd sooner sell you the dorg, sir. 'S trewth I would!"

A shadow fell on the draw-bridge, and
Ortheris began to rise into the air, lifted by
a huge hand upon his collar.

"Onything but t' braass," said Learoyd,
quietly, as he held the Londoner over the
ditch. "Onything but t' braass, Orth'ris,
ma son! Ah've got one rupee eight annas
of ma own." He showed two coins, and re-
placed Ortheris on the draw-bridge rail.

"Very good," I said; "where are you
going to?"

"Goin' to walk 'im orf wen 'e comes out—
two miles or three or fower," said Ortheris.

The footsteps within ceased. I heard the
dull thud of a knapsack falling on a bedstead, followed by the rattle of arms. Ten
minutes later, Mulvaney, faultlessly attired,
his lips compressed and his face as black as
a thunderstorm, stalked into the sunshine
on the draw-bridge. Learoyd and Ortheris
sprung from my side and closed in upon
him, both leaning toward as horses lean
upon the pole. In an instant they had disappeared down the sunken road to the cantonments, and I was left alone. Mulvaney
had not seen fit to recognize me; wherefore,
I felt that his trouble must be heavy upon
him.

I climbed one of the bastions and watched
the figures of the Three Musketeers grow
smaller and smaller across the plain. They
were walking as fast as they could put foot
to the ground, and their heads were bowed.

They fetched a great compass round the parade-ground, skirted the cavalry lines, and vanished in the belt of trees that fringes the low land by the river.

I followed slowly, and sighted them—dusty, sweating, but still keeping up their long, swinging tramp—on the river-bank. They crashed through the forest reserve, headed toward the bridge of boats, and presently established themselves on the brow of the pontoons. I rode cautiously till I saw three puffs of white smoke rise and die out in the clear evening air, and knew that peace had come again. At the bridge-head they waved me forward with gestures of welcome.

"Tie up your 'orse," shouted Ortheris, "an' come on, sir. We're all goin' 'ome in this 'ere bloomin' boat."

From the bridge-head to the forest officers' bungalow is but a step. The mess-man was there, and would see that a man held my horse. Did the sahib require aught else—a peg, or beer? Ritchie Sahib had left half a dozen bottles of the latter, but since the sahib was a friend of Ritchie Sahib, and he, the mess-man, was a poor man—

I gave my order quietly, and returned to the bridge. Mulvaney had taken off his boots, and was dabbling his toes in the water; Learoyd was lying on his back on the pontoon; and Ortheris was pretending to row with a big bamboo.

"I'm an ould fool," said Mulvaney, re-

flectively, " dhraggin' you two out here bekaze I was undher the black dog—sulkin'
like a child. Me that was soldierin' when
Mullins, an' be damned to him, was
shquealin' on a counterpin for foive shillin's
a week, an' that not paid ! Bhoys, I've took
you foive miles out av natural pevarsity.
Phew !"

" Wot's the odds as long as you're 'appy ?"
said Ortheris, applying himself afresh to the
bamboo. " As well 'ere as anywhere else."

Learoyd held up a rupee and an eight
anna bit, and shook his head sorrowfully.
" Five mile from t' canteen, all along o'
Mulvaney's blaasted pride."

" I know ut," said Mulvaney, penitently.
"Why will ye come wid me?   An' yet I wud
be mortial sorry if ye did not—any time—
though I am ould enough to know betther.
But I will do penance.   I will take a dhrink
av water."

Ortheris squeaked shrilly.   The butler of
the forest bungalow was standing near the
railings with a basket, uncertain how to
clamber down to the pontoon.

" Might 'a' know'd you'd 'a' got liquor out
o' a bloomin' desert, sir," said Ortheris, grace-
fully, to me.   Then to the mess-man : " Easy
with them there bottles.   They're worth
their weight in gold.   Jock, ye long-armed
beggar, get out o' that an' hike 'em down."

Learoyd had the basket on the pontoon in
an instant, and the Three Musketeers gath-

ered round it with dry lips. They drank
my health in due and ancient form, and
thereafter tobacco tasted sweeter than
ever. They absorbed all the beer, and disposed themselves in picturesque attitudes to
admire the setting sun—no man speaking
for awhile.

Mulvaney's head dropped upon his chest,
and we thought that he was asleep.

" What on earth did you come so far for ?"
I whispered to Ortheris.

" To walk 'im orf, o' course. When e'es
been checked we allus walks 'im orf. 'E
ain't fit to be spoke to those times—nor 'e
ain't fit to leave alone neither. So we takes
'im till 'e is."

Mulvaney raised his head, and stared
straight into the sunset. " I had my rifle,"
said he, dreamily, " an' I had my bay'nit,
an' Mullins came round the corner, an' he
looked in my face an' grinned dishpiteful.
'You can't blow your own nose,' said he.
Now I can't tell fwhat Mullins's expayrience
may ha' been, but, Mother av God, he was
nearer to his death that minut' than I have
iver been to mine—an' that's less than the
thicknuss av a hair !"

" Yes," said Ortheris, calmly, " you'd look
fine with all your buttons took orf, an' the
band in front o' you, walkin' roun' slow
time. We're both front-rank men, me an'
Jock, when the rig'ment's in hollow square.
Bloomin' fine you'd look. ' The Lord giveth

an' the Lord taketh awai— Heasy with that there drop! Blessed be the naime o' the Lord!'" He gulped in a quiet and suggestive fashion.

"Mullins! Wot's Mullins?" said Learoyd, slowly. "Ah'd take a coomp'ny o' Mullinses—ma hand behind me. Sitha, Mulvaney, dunnat be a fool."

"You were not checked for fwat you did not do, an' made a mock av afther. 'Twas for less than that the Tyrone wud ha' sent O'Hara to hell, instid av lettin' him go by his own choosin' whin Rafferty shot him," retorted Mulvaney.

"And who stopped the Tyrone from doing it?" I asked.

"That ould fool who's sorry he didn't stick the pig Mullins." His head dropped again. When he raised it he shivered and put his hand on the shoulders of his two companions.

"Ye've walked the divil out av me, bhoys," said he.

Ortheris shot out the red-hot dottel of his pipe on the back of the hairy fist. "They say e'll's 'otter than that," said he, as Mulvaney swore aloud. "You be warned so. Look yonder!"—he pointed across the river to a ruined temple—"Me an' you an' 'im" —he indicated me by a jerk of his head— "was there one day when Hi made a bloomin' show o' myself. You an' 'im stopped me doin' such—an' Hi was on'y wishful for to desert. You are makin' a bigger bloomin' show o' yourself now."

" Don't mind him, Mulvaney," I said; " Dinah Shadd won't let you hang yourself yet awhile, and you don't intend to try it either. Let's hear about the Tyrone and O'Hara. Rafferty shot him for fooling with his wife. What happened before that?"

" There's no fool like an ould fool. You know you can do anythin' with me whin I'm talkin'. Did I say I wud like to cut Mullins's liver out? I deny the imputa-shin, for fear that Orth'ris here wud report me—Ah! You wud tip me into the river, wud you? Sit quiet, little man. Any ways, Mullins is not worth the trouble av an extry p'rade, an' I will trate him wid outrajis contimpt. The Tyrone an' O'Hara! O'Hara an' the Tyrone, begad! Ould days are hard to bring back into the mouth, but they're always inside the head."

Followed a long pause.

" O'Hara was a divil. Though I saved him, for the honor av the rig'mint, from his death that time, I say it now. He was a divil—a long, bould, black-haired divil."

" Which way?" asked Ortheris.

" Women."

" Then I know another."

" Not more than in reason, if you mane me, ye warped walkin'-shtick. I have been young, an' for why should I not have tuk what I cud? Did I iver, whin I was cor-

p'ril, use the rise av me rank—wan step an'
that taken away, more's the sorrow an' the
fault av me!—to prosecute a nefarious in-
thrigue, as O'Hara did?  Did I, whin I was
corp'ril, lay me spite upon a man an' make
his life a dog's life from day to day?  Did
I lie, as O'Hara lied, till the young wans in
the Tyrone turned white wid the fear av the
judgmint av God killin' thim all in a lump,
as ut killed the woman at Devizes?  I did
not!  I have sinned me sins an' I have
made me confesshin', an' Father Victor
knows the worst av me.  O'Hara was tuk,
before he cud spake, on Rafferty's door-step,
an' no man knows the worst av him.  But
this much I know!

"The Tyrone was recruited any fashion
in the ould days.  A draf' from Connemara
—a draf' from Portsmouth—a draf' from
Kerry, an' that was a blazin' bad draf'—
here, there an' iverywhere—but the large
av thim was Oirish—Black Oirish.  Now
there are Oirish an' Oirish.  The good are
good as the best, but the bad are wurrst than
the wurrst.  'Tis this way.  They clog together in pieces as fast as thieves, an' no
wan knows fwhat they will do till wan turns
informer an' the gang is bruk.  But ut
begins again, a day later, meetin' in holes
an' corners an' swearin' bloody oaths an'
shtickin' a man in the back an' runnin'
away, an' thin waitin' for the blood-money
on the reward papers—to see if it's worth

enough. Those are the Black Oirish, an'
'tis they that bring dishgrace upon the name
av Oireland, an' thim I wud kill—as I nearly
killed wan wanst.

"But to reshume. Me room—'twas before I was married—was wid twelve av the
scum av the earth—the pickin's av the gutter
—mane men that wud neither laugh nor talk
nor yet get dhrunk as a man shud. They
thried some av their dog thricks on me, but
I dhrew a line round me cot, an' the man
that thransgressed ut wint into hospital for
three days good.

"O'Hara had put his spite on the room—
he was my color-sarjint—an' nuthin' cud we
do to plaze him. I was younger than I am
now, an' I tuk what I got in the way av
dressin' down an' punishmint-dhrill wid
me tongue in me cheek. But it was dif-
f'rint wid the others, an why I can not say,
excipt that some men are borrun mane an'
go to dhirty murdher where a fist is more
than enough. Afther a whoile, they changed
their chune to me an' was desp'rit frien'ly—
all twelve av thim cursin' O'Hara in chorus.

"'Eyah,' sez I, 'O'Hara's a divil and I'm
not for denyin' ut, but is he the only man in
the wurruld? Let him go. He'll get tired
av findin' our kit foul an' our 'couterments
onproperly kep'.'

"'We will not let him go,' sez they.

"'Thin take him,' sez I, 'an' a dashed poor
yield you will get for your throuble.'

" ' Is he not misconductin' himself wid Slimmy's wife ?' sez another.

" ' She's common to the rig'mint,' sez I. 'Fwhat has made ye this partic'lar on a suddint ?'

" ' Has he not put his spite on the roomful av us ? Can we do anythin' that he will not check us for ?' sez another.

" ' That's thrue,' sez I.

" ' Will ye not help us to do aught,' sez another—' a big bould man like you ?'

" ' I will break his head upon his shoulthers av he puts hand on me,' sez I. ' I will give him the lie av he says that I'm dhirty, an' I wud not mind duckin' him in the artillery troughs if ut was not that I'm thryin' for me shtripes.'

" ' Is that all ye will do ?' sez another. ' Have ye no more spunk than that, ye blood-dhrawn calf ?'

" ' Blood-dhrawn I may be,' sez I, gettin' back to me cot an' makin' me line round ut ; ' but ye know that the man who comes acrost this mark will be more blood-dhrawn than me. No man gives me the name in me mouth,' I sez. ' Ondersthand, I will have no part wid you in anythin' ye do, nor will I raise me fist to me shuperior. Is any wan comin' on ?' sez I.

" They made no move, tho' I gave thim full time, but stud growlin' an' snarlin' togither at wan ind av the room. I tuk up me cap an' wint out to canteen, thinkin' no

little av mesilf, an' there I grew most onda-
cintly dhrunk in my legs. Me head was all
reasonable.

" ' Houligan,' I sez to a man In E Com-
p'ny that was by way av bein' a frind av
mine, ' I'm overtuk from the belt down.
Do you give me the touch av your shoulther to presarve me formashun an' march me
acrost the ground into the high grass. I'll
sleep ut off there,' sez I ; an' Houligan—he's
dead now, but good he was while he lasted
—walked wid me, givin' me the touch whin
I wint wide, ontil we came to the high grass,
an', my faith, the sky an' the earth was fair
rowlin' undher me. I made for where the
grass was thickest, an' there I slep' off my
liquor wid an aisy conscience. I did not
desire to come on books too frequint, me
characther havin' been shpotless for the good
half av a year.

" Whin I roused, the dhrink was dyin' out
in me, an' I felt as though a she-cat had lit-
tered in me mouth. I had not learned to
hould me liquor wid comfort in thim days.
'Tis little betther I am now. ' I will get
Houligan to pour a bucket over me head,'
thinks I, an' wud ha' risen, but I heard some
wan say : ' Mulvaney can take the blame av
ut for the backslidin' hound he is.'

" ' Oho !' sez I, an' my head rang like a
guard-room gong; 'fwhat is the blame that
this young man must take to oblige Tim
Vulmea ?' For 'twas Tim Vulmea that

shpoke. " I turned on me belly an' crawled through the grass, a bit at a time, to where the spache came from. There was the twelve av my room sittin' down in a little patch, the dhry grass wavin' above their heads an' the sin av black murdher in their hearts. I put the stuff aside to get a clear view.

"' Fwhat's that?' sez wan man, jumpin' up.

"' A dog,' says Vulmea. 'You're a nice hand to this job! As I said, Mulvaney will take the blame—av ut comes to a pinch.'

"' 'Tis harrd to swear a man's life away,' sez a young wan.

"' Thank ye for that,' thinks I. 'Now, fwhat the divil are you paragins conthrivin' against me?'

"' 'Tis as easy as dhrinkin' your quart,' sez Vulmea. 'At sivin or thereon, O'Hara will come acrost to the married quarters, goin' to call on Slimmy's wife, the swine! Wan av us'll pass the wurrd to the room an' we shtart the divil an' all av a shine— laughin' an' crackin' on an' t'rowin' our boots about. Thin O'Hara will come to give us the ordher to be quiet, the more by token because the room-lamp will be knocked over in the larkin'. He will take the straight road to the ind door where there's the lamp in the veranda, an' that'll bring him clear against the light as he sthands. He will not be able to look into the dhark. Wan av us

will loose off, an' a close shot ut will be, an'
shame to the man that misses. 'Twill be
Mulvaney's rifle, she that is at the head av
the rack—there's no mistakin' that long-
shtocked, cross-eyed bitch even in the
dhark.'

" The thief misnamed me ould firin'-piece
out av jealousy—I was pershuaded av that
—an' ut made me more angry than all.

"But Vulmea goes on: 'O'Hara will
dhrop, an' by the time the light's lit again
there'll be some six av us on the chist av
Mulvaney, cryin' murdher an' rape. Mulvaney's cot is near the ind door, an' the
shmokin' rifle will be lyin' undher him
whin we've knocked him over. We know,
an' all the rig'mint knows, that Mulvaney
has given O'Hara more lip than any man av
us. Will there be any doubt at the coort-
martial?  Wud twelve honust sodger-bhoys
swear away the life av a dear, quiet, swate-
timpered man such as is Mulvaney—wid
his line av pipe-clay roun' his cot, threaten-
in' us wid murdher av we overshtepped ut,
as we can truthful testify?'

"'Mary, Mother av Mercy!' thinks I to
mesilf; 'it is this to have an unruly mimher
an' fistes fit to use! Oh, the sneakin'
hounds!'

" The big dhrops ran down me face, for I
was wake wid the liquor an' had not the
full av me wits about me.  I laid shtill an'
heard thim workin' themselves up to swear

me life by tellin' tales av ivry time I had
put me mark on wan or another; an' my
faith, they was few that was not so dishtin-
guished. 'Twas all in the way av fair fight,
though, for niver did I raise me hand excipt
whin they had provoked me to ut.

"'Tis all well,' sez wan av thim, 'but
who's to do this shootin'?'

"'Fwhat matther?' sez Vulmea. ''Tis
Mulvaney will do that—et the coort-martial.'

"'He will so,' sez the man, 'but whose
hand is put to the trigger—in the room?'

"'Who'll do ut?' sez Vulmea, lookin'
round, but divil a man answered. They
began to dishpute till Kiss, that was always
playin' Shpoil Five, sez: 'Thry the kyards!'
Wid that he opined his jackut an' tuk out
the greasy palammers, an' they all fell in
wid the notion.

"'Deal on!' sez Vulmea, wid a big rattlin'
oath, 'an' the Black Curse av Shielygh come
to the man that will not do his duty as the
kyards say. Amin!'

"'Black Jack is the masther,' sez Kiss,
dealin'. Black Jack, sorr, I shud expaytiate
to you, is the ace of shpades, which from
time immimorial has been intimately connected with battle, murdher an' suddin
death.

"Wanst Kiss dealt an' there was no sign,
but the men was whoit wid the workin's av
their sowls. Twice Kiss dealt, an' there was
a gray shine on their cheeks like the mess av

an egg. Three times Kiss dealt an' they
was blue. ' Have ye not lost him ?' sez Vulmea, wipin' the sweat on him. ' Let's ha'
done quick !' ' Quick ut is,' sez Kiss, t'rowin'
him the kyard ; an' ut fell face on his knee
—Black Jack !

"Thin they all cackled wid laughin'.
' Duty thrippence,' sez wan av thim, ' an'
damned cheap at that price !' But I cud
see they all dhrew a little away from Vulmea
an' lef' him sittin' playin' wid the kyard.
Vulmea sez no word for awhoile but licked
his lips—cat-ways. Thin he threw up his
head an' made the men swear by ivry oath
known an' unknown to stan' by him not
alone in the room but at the coort-martial
that was to set on me ! He tould off five av
the biggest to stretch me on me cot whin the
shot was fired, an' another man he tould
off to put out the light, an' yet another
to load me rifle. He wud not do that himself ; an' that was quare, for 'twas but a little
thing.

"Thin they swore over again that they
wud not bethray wan another, an' crep' out
av the grass in diff'rint ways, two be two.
A mercy ut was that they did not come on
me. I was sick wid fear in the pit av me
stummick—sick, sick, sick ! After they was
all gone, I wint back to the canteen an'
called for a quart to put a thought in me.
Vulmea was there, dhrinkin' heavy, an' politeful to me beyond reason. ' Fwhat will I

do—fwhat will I do?' thinks I to mesilf whin Vulmea wint away.

"Prisintly the arm'rer sarjint comes in stiffin' an' crackin' on, not pleased wid any wan, bekaze the Martini-Henri bein' new to the rig'mint in those days we used to play the mischief wid her arrangemints. 'Twas a long time before I cud get out av the way av thryin' to pull the back-sight an' turnin' her over afther firin'—as if she was a Snider.

"'Fwhat tailor-men do they give me to work wid?' sez the arm'rer sarjint. 'Here's Hogan, his nose flat as a table, laid by for a week, an' ivry comp'ny sendin' their arrums in knocked to small shivreens.'

"'Fwhat's wrong wid Hogan, sarjint?' sez I.

"'Wrong!' sez the arm'rer sarjint; 'I showed him, as though I had been his mother, the way av shtrippin' a 'Tini, an' he shtrup her clane an' aisy. I towld him to put her to again an' fire a blank into the blow-pit to show how the dirt hung on the groovin'. He did that, but he did not put in the pin av the fallin' block, an' av coorse whin he fired he was strook by the block jumpin' clear. Well for him 'twas but a blank—a full charge wud ha' cut his oi out.'

"I looked a trifle wiser than a boiled sheep's head. 'How's that, sarjint?' sez I.

"'This way, ye blundherin' man, an' don't be doin' ut,' sez he. Wid that he shows me a Waster action—the breech av her all cut away to show the inside—an' so plazed was he to grumble that he dimonstrated fwhat Hogan had done twice over. 'An' that comes av not knowin' the wepping you're purvided wid,' sez he.

"'Thank ye, sarjint,' sez I; 'I will come to you again for further informashun.

"'Ye will not,' sez he. 'Kape your clanin'-rod away from the breech-pin or you will get into throuble.'

"I wint outside an' I could ha' danced wid delight for the grandeur av ut. 'They will load me rifle, good luck to thim, whoile I'm away,' thinks I, an' back I wint to the canteen to give them their clear chanst.

"The canteen was fillin' wid men at the ind av the day. I made feign to be far gone in dhrink, an', wan by wan, all my roomful came in wid Vulmea. I wint away, walkin' thick an' heavy, but not so thick an' heavy that any wan cud ha' tuk me. Sure an' thrue, there was a kyartridge gone from my pouch an' lyin' snug in me rifle. I was hot wid rage ag'inst thim all, an' I worried the bullet out wid me teeth as fast as I cud, the room bein' empty. Then I tuk me boot an' the clanin'-rod an' knocked out the pin av the fallin'-block. Oh, 'twas music whin that pin rowled on the flure! I put ut into me pouch an' stuck a dab av dirt on the holes in the plate, puttin' the fallin'-block back. 'That'll do your business, Vulmea, sez I, lyin' easy on the cot. 'Come an' sit on me chest the whole room av you, an' I will take you to me bosom for the biggest divils that iver cheated halter. I wud have no mercy on Vulmea. His oi or his life— little I cared!

"At dusk they came back, the twelve av thim, an' they had all been dhrinkin'. I was shammin' sleep on the cot. Wan man wint outside on the veranda. Whin he whistled they began to rage roun' the room an' carry on tremenjus. But I niver want to hear men laugh as they did—skylarkin' too! 'Twas like mad jackals.

"'Shtop that blasted noise!' sez O'Hara in the dark, an' pop goes the room lamp. I cud hear O'Hara runnin' up an' the rattlin' av my rifle in the rack an' the men breathin' heavy as they stud roun' me cot. I cud see O'Hara in the light av the veranda lamp, an' thin I heard the crack av me rifle. She cried loud, poor darlint, bein' mishandled. Next minut five men were houldin' me down. 'Go easy,' I sez; 'fwhat's ut all about?'

"Thin Vulmea, on the flure, raised a howl you cud hear from wan ind av contonmints to the ither. 'I'm dead, I'm butchered, I'm blind!' sez he. 'Saints have mercy on me sinful sowl! Sind for Father Constant! Oh, sind for Father Constant an' let me go clean!' By that I knew he was not dead as I cud ha' wished.

"O'Hara picks up the lamp in the veranda wid a hand as stiddy as a rest.
'Fwhat damned dog's thrick is this av
yours?' sez he, an' turns the light on Tim
Vulmea that was shwimmin' in blood from
top to toe. The fallin'-block had sprung
free behin' a full charge av powther—good
care I tuk to bite down the brass afther
takin' out the bullet that there might be
somethin' to give ut full worth—an' had cut
Tim from the lip to the corner av the right
eye, lavin' the eyelid in tatthers, an' so up
an' along by the forehead to the hair. 'Twas
more av a rakin' plow, if you will ondherstand, than a clean cut; an' niver did I see
a man bleed as Vulmea did. The dhrink
an' the stew that he was in pumped the
blood strong. The minut the men sittin' on
me chist heard O'Hara spakin' they scatthered each wan to his cot, an' cried out
very politeful: 'Fwhat is ut, sarjint?'

"'Fwhat is ut!' sez O'Hara, shakin' Tim.
'Well an' good do you know fwhat ut is, ye
skulkin' ditch-lurkin' dogs! Get a doolie,
an' take this whimperin' scut away. There
will be more heard av ut than any av you
will care for.'

"Vulmea sat up rockin' his head in his
hand an' moanin' for Father Constant.

"'Be done!' sez O'Hara, dhraggin' him up
by the hair. 'You're none so dead that you
cannot go fifteen years for thryin' to shoot
me.''

" ' I did not,' sez Vulmea ; I was shootin'
mesilf.'

" ' That's quare,' sez O'Hara, ' for the front
av my jackut is black wid your powther.'
He tuk up the rifle that was still warm an'
began to laugh. ' I'll make your life hell
to you,' sez he, ' for attempted murdher an'
kapin' your rifle onproperly. You'll be
hanged first, an' thin put undher stoppages
for four fifteen. The rifle's done for,' sez he.

" ' Why, 'tis my rifle !" sez I, comin' up to
look; ' Vulmea, ye divil, fwhat were you
doin' wid her—answer me that?'

" ' Lave me alone,' sez Vulmea ; ' I'm
dyin' !'

" ' I'll wait till you're betther,' sez I, ' an'
thin we two will talk it out umbrageous.'

" O'Hara pitched Tim into the doolie,
none too tinder, but all the bhoys kep' by
their cots, which was not the sign av innocint men. I was huntin' ivrywhere for me
fallin'-block, but not findin' ut at all. I
niver found ut.

" ' Now fwhat will I do ?' sez O'Hara,
swinging the veranda light in his hand an'
lookin' down the room. I had hate and
contimpt av O'Hara, an' I have now, dead
tho' he is, but, for all that, will I say he was
a brave man. He is baskin' in purgathory
this tide, but I wish he cud hear that, whin
he stud lookin' down the room an' the bhoys
shivered before the oi av him, I knew him
for a brave man an' I liked him so.

" ' Fwhat will I do ?' sez O'Hara ag'in, an' we heard the voice av a woman low and sof' in the veranda. 'Twas Slimmy's wife, come over at the shot, sittin' on wan av the benches an' scarce able to walk.

" ' Oh, Denny—Denny dear,' sez she, ' have they kilt you ?'

" O'Hara looked down the room again an' showed his teeth to the gum. Then he spat on the flure.

" ' You're not worth ut,' sez he. ' Light that lamp, ye dogs,' an' wid that he turned away, an' I saw him walkin' off wid Slim· my's wife, she thryin' to wipe off the pow· ther-black on the front av his jackut wid her handkerchief. ' A brave man you are,' thinks I—' a brave man an' a bad woman.'

" No wan said a word for a time. They was all ashamed, past spache.

" ' Fwhat d'you think he will do ?' sez wan av thim at last. ' He knows we're all in ut.'

" ' Are we so ?' sez I from me cot. ' The man that sez that to me will be hurt. I do not know,' sez I, ' fwhat onderhand divilmint you have conthrived, but by what I've seen I know that you can not commit murdher wid another man's rifle—such shakin' cow-ards you are. I'm goin' to slape.' I sez, ' an' you can blow me head off whoile I lay.' I did not slape, though, for a long time. Can ye wonder?

" Next morn the news was through all the rig'mint, an' there was nothin' that the men did not tell. O'Hara reports, fair an' 'easy, that Vulmea was come to grief through tamperin' wid his rifle in barricks, all for to show the mechanism. An' by me sowl, he had the impart'nince to say that he was on the shpot at the time an' cud certify that ut was an accidint! You might ha' knocked me roomful down wid a straw whin they heard that. 'Twas lucky for thim that the bhoys were always thryin' to find out how the new rifle was made, an' a lot av thim had come up for easin' the pull by shtickin' bits of grass an' such in the part av the lock that showed near the thrigger. The first issues of the 'Tinis was not covered in, an' I mesilf have eased the pull av mine time an' ag'in. A light pull is ten points on the range to me.

"' I will not have this foolishness!' sez the colonel. ' I will twist the tail of Vulmea!' sez he; but whin he saw him, all tied up an' groanin' in hospital, he changed his mind. ' Make him an early convalescint,' sez he to the doctor, an' Vulmea was made so for a warnin'. His big bloody bandages an' face puckered up to wan side did more to kape the bhoys from messin' wid the insides av their rifles than any punishment.

"O'Hara gave no reason for fwhat he'd said, an' all my roomful were too glad to inquire tho' he put his spite upon thim more wearin' than before. Wan day, howiver, he tuk me apart very polite, for he cud be that at the choosin'.

"' You're a good sodger, tho' you're a damned insolint man,' sez he.

"' Fair words, sarjint,' sez I, 'or I may be insolint ag'in.'

"' 'Tis not like you,' sez he, 'to lave your rifle in the rack widout the breech-pin, for widout the breech-pin she was whin Vulmea fired. I should ha' found the break av ut in the eyes av the holes, else,' he sez.

"' Sarjint,' sez I, 'fwhat wud your life ha' been worth av the breech-pin had been in place, for, on me sowl, me life wud be worth just as much to me av I towld you whether ut was or was not. Be thankful the bullet was not there,' I sez.

"' That's thrue,' sez he, pullin' his mus-tache; ' but I do not believe that you, for all your lip, was in that business.'

"' Sarjint,' sez I, ' I cud hammer the life out av a man in ten minuts wid my fistes if that man dishpleased me; for I am a good sodger, an' I will be threated as such, an' whoile me fistes are me own they're strong enough for all work I have to do. They do not fly back towards me!' sez I, lookin' him betune the eyes.

"' You're a good man,' sez he, lookin' me betune the eyes—an' oh, he was a gran' built man to see—'you're a good man,' sez he, ' an' I cud wish, for the pure frolic av ut, that I was not a sarjint, or that you were

not a privit; an' you will think me no cow-
ard whin I say this thing.'

"'I do not,' sez I. 'I saw you whin Vulmea mishandled the rifle. But, sarjint,' I
sez, 'take the wurrd from me now, spakin'
as man to man wid the shtripes off, tho' 'tis
little right I have to talk, me bein' fwhat I
am by natur'. This time ye tuk no harm,
an' next time ye may not, but, in the ind,
so sure as Slimmy's wife came into the veranda, so sure will ye take harm—an' bad
harm. Have thought, sarjint,' sez I. 'Is
ut worth ut?'

"'Ye're a bowld man,' sez he, breathin'
harrd. 'A very bowld man. But I am a
bowld man tu. Do you go your way, Privit
Mulvaney, an' I will go mine.'

"We had no further spache thin or afther,
but, wan by another, he drafted the twelve
av my room out into other rooms an' got
thim spread among the comp'nies, for they
was not a good breed to live together, an' the
comp'ny orf'cers saw ut. They wud ha'
shot me in the night av they had known
fwhat I knew; but they did not.

"An', in the ind, as I said, O'Hara met
his death from Rafferty for foolin' wid his
wife. He wint his own way too well—Eyah,
too well! Shtraight to that affair, widout
turnin' to the right or to the lef', he wint,
an' may the Lord have mercy on his sowl.
Amin!"

"''Ear! 'Ear!" said Ortheris, pointing the

moral with a wave of his pipe. " An' this is
'im 'oo would be a bloomin' Vulmea all for
the sake of Mullins an' a bloomin' button!
Mullins never went after a woman in his
life. Mrs. Mullins, she saw 'im one day—"

"Ortheris," I said, hastily, for the ro-
mances of Private Ortheris are slightly too
daring for publication, "look at the sun.
It's a quarter past six!"

"Oh, Lord! Three quarters of an hour
for five an' a 'arf miles! We'll 'ave to run
like Jimmy O."

The Three Musketeers clambered on to
the bridge, and departed hastily in the direction of the cantonment road. When I
overtook them I offered them two stirrups
and a tail, which they accepted enthusiasti-
cally. Ortheris held the tail, and in this
manner we trotted steadily through the
shadows by the unfrequented road.

At the turn into the cantonments we heard
carriage wheels. It was the colonel's ba-
rouche, and in it sat the colonel's wife and
daughter. I caught a suppressed chuckle,
and my beast sprung forward with a lighter
step.

The Three Musketeers had vanished into
the night.

# THE INCARNATION OF KRISHNA MULVANEY.

ONCE upon a time, and very far from this land, lived three men who loved each other so greatly that neither man nor woman could come between them. They were in no sense refined, not to be admitted to the outer door-mats of decent folk, because they happened to be private soldiers in her majesty's army; and private soldiers of that employ have small time for self-culture. Their duty is to keep themselves and their accoutrements specklessly clean, to refrain from getting drunk more often than is necessary, to obey their superiors, and to pray for a war. All these things my friends accomplished; and of their own motion threw in some fighting work for which the army regulations did not call. Their fate sent them to serve in India, which is not a golden country, though poets have sung otherwise. There men die with great swiftness, and those who live suffer many and curious things. I do not think that my friends concerned themselves much with the social or political aspects of the East. They attended a not unimportant war on the northern frontier, another one on our western bound-

( 137 )

ary, and a third in Upper Burma. Then their regiment sat still to recruit, and the boundless monotony of cantonment life was their portion. They were drilled morning and evening on the same dusty parade-ground. They wandered up and down the same stretch of dusty white road, attended the same church and the same grog-shop, and slept in the same lime-washed barn of a barrack for two long years. There was Mulvaney, the father in the craft, who had served with various regiments from Bermuda to Halifax, old in war, scarred, reckless, resourceful, and in his pious hours an unequalled soldier. To him turned for help and comfort six and a half feet of slow-moving, heavy-footed Yorkshireman, born on the wolds, bred in the dales, and educated chiefly among the carriers' carts at the back of York railway station. His name was Learoyd, and his chief virtue an unmitigated patience which helped him to win fights. How Ortheris, a fox-terrier of a cockney, ever came to be one of the trio, is a mystery which even to-day I can not explain. "There was always three av us," Mulvaney used to say. "An' by the grace av God, so long as our service lasts, three av us they'll always be. 'Tis betther so."

They desired no companionship beyond their own, and evil it was for any man of the regiment who attempted dispute with them. Physical argument was out of the question as regarded Mulvaney and the Yorkshireman; and assault on Ortheris meant a combined attack from these twain —a business which no five men were anxious to have on their hands. Therefore they flourished, sharing their drinks, their tobacco, and their money; good luck and evil; battle and the chances of death; life and the chances of happiness from Calicut in southern, to Peshawur in northern India. Through no merit of my own it was my good fortune to be in a measure admitted to their friendship—frankly by Mulvaney from the beginning, sullenly and with reluctance by Learoyd, and suspiciously by Ortheris, who held to it that no man not in the army could fraternize with a red-coat. "Like to like," said he. "I'm a bloomin' sodger— he's a bloomin' civilian. 'Tain't natural— that's all."

But that was not all. They thawed progressively, and in the thawing told me more of their lives and adventures than I am likely to find room for here.

Omitting all else, this tale begins with the Lamentable Thirst that was at the beginning of First Causes. Never was such a thirst— Mulvaney told me so. They kicked against their compulsory virtue, but the attempt was only successful in the case of Ortheris. He, whose talents were many, went forth into the highways and stole a dog from a " civilian "—*videlicet*, some one, he knew not who, not in the army. Now that civilian was but newly connected by marriage with the colonel of the regiment, and outcry was made from quarters least anticipated by Ortheris, and in the end he was forced, lest a worse thing should happen, to dispose at ridiculously unremunerative rates of as promising a small terrier as ever graced one end of a leading-string. The purchase money was barely sufficient for one small outbreak which led him to the guard-room. He escaped, however, with nothing worse than a severe reprimand and a few hours of punishment drill. Not for nothing had he acquired the reputation of being "the best soldier of his inches" in the regiment. Mulvaney had taught personal cleanliness and efficiency as the first articles of his companions' creed. "A dhirty man," he was used to say, in the speech of his kind, "goes to clink for a weakness in the knees, an' is coort-martialed for a pair av socks missin'; but a clane man, such as is an ornament to his service—a man whose buttons are gold, whose coat is wax upon him, an'•whose 'couterments are widout a speck—*that* man may, spakin' in reason, do fwhat he likes an' dhrink from day to divil. That's the pride av bein' dacint."

We sat together upon a day, in the shade of a ravine far from the barracks, where a water-course used to run in rainy weather. Behind us was the scrub jungle, in which jackalls, peacocks, the gray wolves of the North-western Provinces, and occasionally a tiger estrayed from Central India, were supposed to dwell. In front lay the cantonment, white under a glaring sun, and on either side ran the broad road that led to Delhi.

It was the scrub that suggested to my mind the wisdom of Mulvaney taking a day's leave and going upon a shooting-tour. The peacock is a holy bird throughout India, and whoso slays one is in danger of being mobbed by the nearest villagers; but on the last occasion that Mulvaney had gone forth he had contrived, without in the least offending local religious susceptibilities, to return with six beautiful peacock skins which he sold to profit. It seemed just possible then—

"But fwhat manner ave use is ut to me goin' out widout a dhrink? The ground's powdher-dhry under-foot, an' ut gets unto the throat fit to kill," wailed Mulvaney, looking at me reproachfully. "An' a peacock is not a bird you can catch the tail av onless ye run. Can a man run on wather—an' jungle-wather too?"

Ortheris had considered the question in all its bearings. He spoke, chewing his pipe-stem meditatively the while:

"'Go forth, return in glory,
  To Clusium's royal 'ome:
  An' round these bloomin' temples 'ang
  The bloomin' shields o' Rome.'

You better go.   You ain't like to shoot yourself—not while there's a chanst of liquor.
Me an' Learoyd 'll stay at 'ome an' keep
shop—case o' anythin' turnin' up.   But you
go out with a gas pipe gun an' ketch the
little peacockses or somethin'.   You kin
get one day's leave easy as winkin'.   Go
along an' get it, an' get peacockses or somethin'."

"Jock?" said Mulvaney, turning to Learoyd, who was half asleep under the shadow
of the bank.   He roused slowly.

"Sitha, Mulvaney, go," said he.

And Mulvaney went; cursing his allies
with Irish fluency and barrack room point.

"Take note," said he, when he had won
his holiday, and appeared dressed in his
roughest clothes with the only other regi-
mental fowling-piece in his hand—"take
note, Jock, an' you, Orth'ris, I am goin' in
the face av my own will—all for to please
you.   I misdoubt anythin' will come av per-
nicious huntin' afther peacockses in a deso-
lit lan'; an' I know that I will lie down an'
die wid thirrst.   Me catch peacockses for you,
ye lazy scutts—an' be sacrificed by the
peasanthry—Ugh!"

He waved a huge paw and went away.

At twilight, long before the appointed
hour, he returned empty-handed, much be-
grimed with dirt.

"Peacockses?" queried Ortheris, from the
safe rest of a barrack-room table whereon

he was smoking cross-legged, Learoyd fast asleep on a bench.

"Jock," said Mulvaney without answering, as he stirred up the sleeper. "Jock, can ye fight? Will ye fight?"

Very slowly the meaning of the words communicated itself to the half-roused man. He understood—and again—what might these things mean? Mulvaney was shaking him savagely. Meantime the men in the room howled with delight. There was war in the confederacy at last—war and the breaking of bonds.

Barrack-room etiquette is stringent. On the direct challenge must follow the direct reply. This is more binding than the ties of tried friendship. Once again Mulvaney repeated the question. Learoyd answered by the only means in his power, and so swiftly that the Irishman had barely time to avoid the blow. The laughter around increased. Learoyd looked bewildered at his friend—himself as greatly bewildered. Ortheris dropped from the table because his world was falling.

"Come outside," said Mulvaney, and as the occupants of the barrack-room prepared joyously to follow, he turned and said furiously: "There will be no fight this night—onless any wan av you is wishful to assist. The man that does, follow on."

No man moved. The three passed out into the moonlight, Learoyd fumbling with the buttons of his coat. The parade-ground was deserted except for the scurrying jackals. Mulvaney's impetuous rush carried his companions far into the open ere Learoyd attempted to turn round and continue the discussion.

"Be still now. 'Twas my fault for beginin' things in the middle av an end, Jock. I should ha' comminst wid an explanion; but Jock, dear, on your sowl are ye fit, think you, for the finest fight that iver was—betther than fightin' me? Considher before ye answer."

More than ever puzzled, Learoyd turned round two or three times, felt an arm, kicked tentatively, and answered, "Ah'm fit." He was accustomed to fight blindly at the bidding of the superior mind.

They sat them down, the men looking on from afar, and Mulvaney untangled himself in mighty words.

"Followin' your fools' scheme I wint out into the thrackless desert beyond the barricks. An' there I met a pious Hindu dhriving' a bullock-kyart. I tuk ut for granted he wud be delighted for to convoy me a piece, an' I jumped in—"

"You long, lazy, black-haired swine," drawled Ortheris, who would have done the same thing under similar circumstances.

"'Twas the height av policy. That naygur-man dhruv miles an' miles—as far as the new railway line they're buildin' now back av the Tavi River. ' 'Tis a kyart for dhirt only,' say he now an' again, timoreously, to get me out av ut. 'Dhirt I am,' sez I, ' an' the dhryest that you iver kyarted. Dhrive on, me son, an' glory be wid you.' At that I wint to slape, an' took no heed till he pulled up on the embankmint av the line where the coolies were pilin' mud. There was a matther av two thousand coolies on that line—you remimber that. Prisintly a bell rang, an' they throops off to a big pay-shed. 'Where's the white man in charge?' sez I to my kyart-dhriver. ' In the shed,'sez he, ' engaged on a riffle.' ' A fwhat?' sez I. ' Riffle,' sez he. ' You take ticket. He take money. You get nothin'.' ' Oho!' sez I, ' that's fwhat the shuper'or an' cultivated man calls a raffle, me misbeguided child av darkness an' sin. Lead on to that raffle, though fwhat the mischief 'tis doin' so far away from uts home—which is the charity-bazaar at Christmas, an' the colonel's wife grinnin' behind the tea-table—is more than I know.' Wid that I wint to the shed an' found 'twas pay-day among the coolies. Their wages was on a table forninst a big, fine, red buck av a man—sivin fut high, four fut wide, an' three fut thick, wid a fist on him like a corn-sack. He was payin' the coolies fair an' easy, but he wud ask each man if he wud raffle that month, an'each man sez, ' Yes,' av course. Thin he wud deduct from their wages accordin'. Whin all was

paid, he filled an' ould cigar-box full av
gun-wads an' scatthered ut among the coolies. They did not take much joy av that
performance, an' small wondher. A man
close to me picks up a black gun-wad an'
sings out, 'I have ut.' 'Good may ut do
you,' sez I. The coolie wint forward to the
big, fine, red man, who threw a cloth off the
most sumpshus, jooled, enameled, an' vari-
ously bediviled sedan-chair I iver saw."

"Sedan-chair! Put your 'ead in a bag.
That was a palanquin. Don't yer know a
palanquin when you see it?" said Ortheris,
with great scorn.

" I chuse to call ut sedan-chair, an' chair
ut shall be, little man," continued the Irishman. "'Twas a most amazin' chair—all
lined wid pink silk an' fitted wid red silk
curtains. 'Here ut is,' sez the red man.
'Here ut is,' sez the coolie, an' he grinned
weakly-ways. 'Is ut any use to you?' sez
the red man. 'No,' sez the coolie; 'I'd like
to make a presint av ut to you.' 'I am
graciously pleased to accept that same,' sez
the red man, 'an' at that all the coolies
cried aloud in fwhat was mint for cheerful
notes, an' wint back to their diggin', lavin'
me alone in the shed. The red man saw
me, an' his face grew blue on his big, fat
neck. 'Fwhat d'you want here?' sez he.
'Standin'-room an' no more,' sez I, 'onless
it may be fwhat ye niver had, an' that's
manners, ye rafflin' ruffian,' for I was not

goin' to have the service throd upon. 'Out of this,' sez he. 'I'm in charge av this section av construction.' 'I'm in charge av mesilf,' sez I, 'an' it's like I will stay awhile. D'ye raffle much in these parts?' 'Fwhat's that to you?' sez he. 'Nothin', sez I, 'but a great dale to you, for begad I'm thinkin' you get the full half av your revenue from that sedan-chair. Is ut always raffled so?' I sez, an' wid that I wint to a coolie to ask questions. Bhoys, that man's name is Dearsley, an' he's been rafflin' that old sedan-chair monthly this matter av nine months. Ivry coolie on the section takes a ticket—or he gives 'em the go—wanst a month on pay-day. Ivry coolie that wins ut gives ut back to him, for 'tis too big to carry away, an he'd sack the man that thried to sell ut. That Dearsley has been makin' the rowlin' wealth av Roshus by nefarious rafflin'. Think av the burnin' shame to the sufferin' coolie-man that the army in Injia are bound to protect an' nourish in their bosoms! Two thousand coolies defrauded wanst a month!"

"Dom t'coolies. Hast gotten t' cheer, man?" said Learoyd.

"Hould on. Havin' onearthed this amazin' an' stupenjus fraud committed by the man Dearsley, I hild a council av war, he thryin' all the time to sejuce me into a fight wid opprobrious language. That sedan-chair niver belonged by right to any foreman av coolies. 'Tis a king's chair or a quane's.

There's gold on ut an' silk an' all manner of trapesemints. Bhoys, 'tis not for me to countenance any sort av wrong-doin'—me bein' the ould man—but—any way he has had ut nine months, an' he dare not make throuble av ut was taken from him. Five miles away, or ut may be six—"

There was a long pause, and the jackals howled merrily. Learoyd bared one arm, and contemplated it in the moonlight. Then he nodded partly to himself and partly to his friends. Ortheris wriggled with suppressed emotion.

" I thought ye wud see the reasonableness av ut," said Mulvaney. " I made bould to say as much to the man before. He was for a direct front attack—fut, horse, an' guns—an' all for nothin,' seein' that I had no thransport to convey the machine away. ' I will not argue wid you,' sez I, ' this day. but subsequintly, Mister Dearsley, me rafflin' jool, we talk ut out lengthways. 'Tis no good policy to swindle the naygur av his hard-earned emolumints, an' by presint informashin'—'twas the kyart-man that tould me—' ye've been perpethrating that same for nine months. But I'm a just man,' sez I, ' an' overlookin' the presumpshin that yondher settee wid the gilt top was not kem by honust'—at that he turned sky-green, so I knew things was more thrue than tellable— 'not kem by honust, I'm willin' to compound the felony for this month's winnin's.' "

"Ah! Ho!" from Learoyd and Ortheris.

"That man Dearsley's rushin' on his fate," continued Mulvaney, solemnly wagging his head. "All hell had no name bad enough for me that tide. Faith, he called me a robber! Me! that was savin' him from continuin' in his evil ways widout a remonstrince—an' to a man av conscience a remonstrince may change the chune av his life. ''Tis not for me to argue,' sez I, 'fwhatever ye are, Mister Dearsley, but by me hand I'll take away the timptation for you that lies in that sedan chair.' 'You will have to fight me for ut,' sez he, ' for well I know you will never dare make report to any one.' ' Fight I will,' sez I, ' but not this day, for I'm rejuced for want av nourishment.' ' Ye're an ould, bould hand,' sez he, sizin' me up an' down; ' an' a jool av a fight we will have. Eat now an' dhrink, an' go your way.' Wid that he gave me some hump an' whisky—good whisky—an' we talked av this an' that the while. 'It goes hard on me now,' sez I, wipin' me mouth, ' to confiscate that piece av furniture, but justice is justice.' ' Ye've not got ut yet,' sez he; 'there's the fight between.' ' There is,' sez I, ' an' a good fight. Ye shall have the pick av the best quality in my rig'mint for the dinner you have given this day.' Thin I came hot-foot to you two. Hould your tongue, the both. 'Tis this way. To-morrow we three will go there an' he shall have his pick betune me an' Jock. Jock's a deceivin' fighter, for he is all fat to the eye, an' he moves slow. Now I'm all beef to the look, an' I move quick. By me reckonin' the Dearsley man won't take me; so me an' Orth'ris 'll see fair play. Jock, I tell you, 'twill be big fightin'—whipped, with the cream above the jam. Afther the business 'twill take a good three av us—Jock 'll be very hurt—to take away that sedan-chair."

"Palanquin." This from Ortheris.

" Fwhatever ut is, we must have ut. 'Tis the only sellin' piece av property widin reach that we can get so cheap. An' fwhat's a fight, afther all? He has robbed the naygur-man, dishonust. We rob him honust for the sake av the whisky he gave me."

" But wot'll we do with the bloomin' harticle when we've got it? Them palanquins are as big as 'ouses, an' uncommon 'ard to sell, as McCleary said when he stole the sentry-box from the Curragh."

" Who's goin' to do t' fightin'?" said Learoyd, and Ortheris subsided. The three returned to barracks without a word. Mulvany's last argument clinched the matter. The palanquin was property, vendible and to be attained in the simplest and least embarrassing fashion. It would eventually become beer. Great was Mulvaney.

Next afternoon a procession of three formed itself and disappeared into the scrub in the direction of the new railway line.

Learoyd alone was without care, for Mulvaney dived darkly into the future, and little Ortherus- feared the unknown. What befell at that interview in the lonely payshed by the side of the half-built embankment only a few hundred coolies know, and their tale is a confusing one, running thus:

"We were at work. Three men in red coats came. They saw the sahib—Dearsley Sahib. They made oration, and noticeably the small man among the red-coats. Dearsley Sahib also made oration, and used many very strong words. Upon this talk they departed together to an open space, and there the fat man in the red coat fought with Dearsley Sahib after the custom of white men—with his hands, making no noise, and never at all pulling Dearsley Sahib's hair. Such of us as were not afraid beheld these things for just so long a time as a man needs to cook the midday meal. The small man in the red coat had possessed himself of Dearsley Sahib's watch. No, he did not steal that watch. He held it in his hand, and at certain seasons made outcry, and the twain ceased their combat, which was like the combat of young bulls in spring. Both men were soon all red, but Dearsley Sahib was much more red than the other. Seeing this, and fearing for his life—because we greatly loved him—some fifty of us made shift to rush upon the red-coats. But a certain man—very black as to the hair, and in no way to be confused with the small man, or the fat man who fought—that man, we affirm, ran upon us, and of us he embraced some ten or fifty in both arms, and beat our heads together, so that our livers turned to water, and we ran away. It is not good to interfere in the fightings of white men. After that Dearsley Sahib fell and did not rise, these men jumped upon his stomach and despoiled him of all his money, and attempted to fire the pay-shed, and departed. Is it true that Dearsley Sahib makes no complaint of these latter things having been done? We were senseless with fear, and do not at all remember. There was no palanquin near the pay-shed. What do we know about palanquins? Is it true that Dearsley Sahib does not return to his place, on account of his sickness, for ten days? This is the fault of those bad men in the red coats, who should be severely punished; for Dearsley Sahib is both our father and mother, and we love him much. Yet, if Dearsley Sahib does not return to this place at all, we will speak the truth. There was a palanquin, for the up-keep of which we were forced to pay nine-tenths of our monthly wage. On such mulctings Dearsley Sahib allowed us to make obeisance to him before the palanquin. What could we do? We were poor men. He took a full half of our wages. Will the government repay us those moneys? Those three men in red coats

bore the palanquin upon their shoulders
and departed. All the money that Dearsley
Sahib had taken from us was in the cushions
of that palanquin. Therefore they stole it.
Thousands of rupees were there—all our
money. It was our bank-box, to fill which
we cheerfully contributed to Dearsley Sahib
three-sevenths of our monthly wage. Why
does the white man look upon us with the
eye of disfavor? Before God, there was a
palanquin, and now there is no palanquin;
and if they send the police here to make in-
quisition, we can only say that there never
has been any palanquin. Why should a
palanquin be near these works? We are
poor men, and we know nothing."

Such is the simplest version of the simplest story connected with the descent upon
Dearsley. From the lips of the coolies I received it. Dearsley himself was in no condition to say anything, and Mulvaney preserved a massive silence, broken only by
the occasional licking of the lips. He had
seen a fight so gorgeous that even his power
of speech was taken from him. I respected
that reserve until, three days after the affair,
I discovered in a disused stable in my quarters a palanquin of unchastened splendor—
evidently in past days the litter of a queen.
The pole whereby it swung between the
shoulders of the bearers was rich with the
painted *papier-maché* of Cashmere. The
shoulder-pads were of yellow silk. The

panels of the litter itself were ablaze with
the loves of all the gods and goddesses of the
Hindu Pantheon—lacquer on cedar. The
cedar sliding-doors were fitted with hasps
of translucent Jaipur enamel, and ran in
grooves shod with silver. The cushions were
of brocaded Delhi silk, and the curtains,
which once hid any glimpse of the beauty
of the king's palace, were stiff with gold.
Closer investigation showed that the entire
fabric was everywhere rubbed and discolored
by time and wear ; but even thus it was
sufficiently gorgeous to deserve housing on
the threshold of a royal zenana. I found no
fault with it, except that it was in my stable.
Then, trying to lift it by the silver-shod
shoulder-pole, I laughed. The road from
Dearsley's pay-shed to the cantonment was
a narrow and uneven one, and, traversed by
three very inexperienced palanquin-bearers,
one of whom was sorely battered about the
head, must have been a path of torment.
Still I did not quite recognize the right of
the three musketeers to turn me into a
"fence " for stolen property.

"I'm askin' you to warehouse ut," said
Mulvaney when he was brought to consider
the question. "There's no steal in ut.
Dearsley tould us we cud have ut if we
fought. Jock fought—an' oh, sorr, when
the throuble was ut its finest an' Jock was
bleedin' like a stuck pig, and little Orth'ris
was shquealin' on one leg chewin' big bites

out av Dearsley's watch, I wud ha' given my place at the fight to have had you see wan round. He tuk Jock, as I suspicioned he would, an' Jock was deceptive. Nine roun's they were even matched, an' at the tenth— About that palanquin now. There's not the least throuble in the world, or we wud not ha' brought ut here. You will on-dherstand that the queen—God bless her!— does not reckon for a privit soldier to kape elephints an' palanquins an' sich in bar-ricks. Afther we had dhragged ut down from Dearsley's through that cruel scrub that near broke Orth'ris's heart, we set ut in the ravine for a night; an' a thief av a por-cupine an' a civet av a jackal roosted in ut, as well we knew in the mornin'. I put ut to you, sorr, is an elegant palanquin, fit for the princess, the natural abidin'-place av all the vermin in cantonmints? We brought ut to you, afther dhark, and put ut in your shtable. Do not let your conscience prick. Think av the rejoicin' men in the pay-shed yonder—lookin' at Dearsley wid his head tied up in a towel—an' well knowin' that they can dhraw their pay ivry month widout stoppages for riffles. Indirectly, sorr, you have rescued from an onprincipled son of a night-hawk the peasanthry av a numerous village. An', besides, will I let that sedan-chair rot on our hands? Not I. 'Tis not every day a piece av pure joolry comes into the market. There's not a king widin these forty miles"—he waved his hand around the dusty horizon—'not a king wud not be glad to buy ut. Some day mesilf, whin I have leisure, I'll take ut up along the road an' dishpose av ut."

"How?" said I, for I knew the man was capable of anything.

"Get into ut, av coorse, an' keep wan eye open through the curtains. Whin I see a likely man av the native persuasion, I will discind blushin' from me canopy an' say: 'Buy a palanquin, ye black scutt?' I will have to hire four men to carry me first, though and that's impossible till next pay-day."

Curiously enough, Learoyd, who had fought for the prize, and in winning secured the highest pleasure life had to offer him, was altogether disposed to undervalue it, while Ortheris openly said that it would be better to break the thing up. Dearsley, he argued, might be a many-sided man, capable, despite his magnificent fighting qualities, of setting in motion the machinery of the civil law—a thing much abhorred by the soldier. Under any circumstances their fun had come and passed; the next pay-day was close a hand, when there would be beer for all. Wherefore longer conserve the painted palanquin?

"A first-class rifle-shot, an' a good little man av your inches you are," said Mulvaney. "But you niver had a head worth a soft-

boiled egg. 'Tis me has to lie awake av
nights schamin' an' plottin' for the three av
us. Orth'ris, me son, 'tis no matther av a
few gallons av beer—no, nor twinty gallons
—but tubs an' vats an' firkins in that sedan-
chair. Who ut was, an' what ut was, an'
how ut got there, we do not know; but I
know in me bones that you an' me an' Jock
wid his sprained thumb will get a fortune
thereby. Lave me alone, an' let me think."

Meantime the palanquin stayed in my
stall, the key of which was in Mulvaney's
hands.

Pay-day came, and with it beer. It was
not in experience to hope that Mulvaney,
dried by four weeks' drought, would avoid
excess. Next morning he and the palanquin had disappeared. He had taken the
precaution of getting three days' leave "to
see a friend on the railway," and the colonel, well knowing that the seasonal out-
burst was near, and hoping it would spend
its force beyond the limits of his jurisdic-
tion, cheerfully gave him all he demanded.
At this point his history, as recorded in the
mess-room, stopped.

Ortheris carried it not much further.
"No, 'e wasn't drunk," said the little man,
loyally, "the liquor was no more than feelin' its way round inside of 'im; but 'e went
an' filled that 'ole bloomin' palanquin with
bottles 'fore 'e went off. He's gone 'an 'ired
six men to carry 'im, an' I 'ad to 'elp 'im

into 'is nupshal couch, 'cause 'e wouldn't 'ear reason. 'E's gone off in 'is shirt an' trousies, swearin' tremenjus—gone down the road in the palanquin, wavin' 'is legs out o' the windy."

" Yes," said I, " but where?"

" Now you arx me a question. 'E said 'e was goin' to sell that palanquin, but from observations what happened when I was stuffin' 'im through the door, I fancy 'e's gone to the new embankment to mock at Dearsley. Soon as Jock's off duty I'm goin' there to see if 'e's safe—not Mulvaney, but t'other man. My saints but I pity 'im as 'elps Terence out o' the palanquin when 'e's once fair drunk!"

" He'll come back without harm," I said.

" 'Corse 'e will. On'y question is, what 'il 'e be doin' on the road. Killin' Dearsley, like as not. 'E shouldn't 'a' gone without Jock or me."

Reinforced by Learoyd, Ortheris sought the foreman of the coolie gang. Dearsley's head was still embellished with towels. Mulvaney, drunk or sober, would have struck no man in that condition, and Dearsley indignantly denied that he would have taken advantage of the intoxicated brave.

" I had my pick o' you two," he explained to Learoyd, " and you got my palanquin— not before I'd made my profit on it. Why'd I do any harm when everything's settled? Your man *did* come here—drunk as Davy's

sow on a frosty night—came a-purpose to
mock me—stuck his head out o' the door an'
called me a crucified hodman. I made him
drunker, an' sent him along. But I never
touched him."

To these things Learoyd, slow to perceive
the evidences of sincerity, answered only,
" If owt comes to Mulvaney 'long o' you,
I'll gripple you, clouts or no clouts on your
ugly head, an' I'll draw t' throat twisty-
ways, man. See there now."

The embassy removed itself, and Dearsley, the battered, laughed alone over his
supper that evening.

Three days passed—a fourth and a fifth.
The week drew to a close and Mulvaney did
not return. He, his royal palanquin, and
his six attendants had vanished into air. A
very large and very tipsy soldier, his feet
sticking out of the litter of a reigning princess, is not a thing to travel along the ways
without comment. Yet no man of all the
country round had seen any such wonder.
He was, and he was not; and Learoyd suggested the immediate smashment of Dearsley as a sacrifice to his ghost. Ortheris
insisted that all was well, and in the light of
past experience his hopes seemed reasonable.

" When Mulvaney goes up the road," said
he, " 'e's like to go a very long ways up,
specially when 'e's so blue drunk as 'e is
now. But what gits me is 'is not bein'
'eared of pullin' wool off the niggers some-

wheres about. That don't look good. The drink must ha' died out in 'im by this, unless 'e's broke a bank, an then— Why don't 'e come back? 'E didn't ought to ha' gone off without us."

Even Ortheris's heart sunk at the end of the seventh day, for half the regiment were out scouring the country-side, and Learoyd had been forced to fight two men who hinted openly that Mulvaney had deserted. To do him justice, the colonel laughed at the notion, even when it was put forward by his much-trusted adjutant.

" Mulvaney would as soon think of deserting as you would," said he. " No, he's either fallen into a mischief among the villagers— and yet that isn't likely, for he'd blarney himself out of the Pit; or else he is engaged on urgent private affairs—some stupendous devilment that we shall hear of at mess after it has been the round of the barrack-rooms. The worst of it is that I shall have to give him twenty-eight days' confinement at least for being absent without leave, just when I most want him to lick the new batch of recruits into shape. I never knew a man who could put a polish on young soldiers as quickly as Mulvaney can. How does he do it?"

" With blarney and the buckle-end of a belt, sir," said the adjutant. " He is worth a couple of non-commissioned officers when we are dealin' with an Irish draft, and the

London lads seem to adore him. The worst
of it is that if he goes to the cells the other
two are neither to hold nor to bind till he
comes out again. I believe Ortheris preaches
mutiny on those occasions, and I know that
the mere presence of Learoyd mourning
for Mulvaney kills all the cheerfulness of
his room. The sergeant tells me that he
allows no man to laugh when he feels un-
happy. They are a queer gang."

"For all that, I wish we had a few more
of them. I like a well-conducted regiment,
but these pasty-faced, shifty-eyed, mealy-
mouthed young slouchers from the depot
worry me sometimes with their offensive
virtue. They don't seem to have backbone
enough to do anything but play cards and
prowl round the married quarters. I believe
I'd forgive that old villain on the spot if he
turned up with any sort of explanation that
I could in decency accept."

"Not likely to be much difficulty about
that, sir," said the adjutant. "Mulvaney's ex-
planations are only one degree less wonderful
than his performances. They say that when
he was in the Black Tyrone, before he came
to us, he was discovered on the banks of the
Liffy trying to sell his colonel's charger to a
Donegal dealer as a perfect lady's hack.
Shackbolt commanded the Tyrone then."

"Shackbolt must have had apoplexy at
the thought of his ramping war-horse answering to that description. He used to

11

buy unbacked devils, and tame them by some pet theory of starvation. What did Mulvaney say?"

"That he was a member of the Society for the Prevention of Cruelty to Animals, anxious to 'sell the poor baste where he would get something to fill out his dimples.' Shackbolt laughed, but I fancy that was why Mulvaney exchanged to ours."

"I wish he were back," said the colonel; "for I like him and believe he likes me."

That evening, to cheer our souls, Learoyd, Ortheris and I went into the waste to smoke out a porcupine. All the dogs attended, but even their clamor—and they began to discuss the shortcomings of porcupines before they left cantonments—could not take us out of ourselves. A large, low moon turned the tops of the plume-grass to silver, and the stunted camel thorn-bushes and sour tamarisks into the likenesses of trooping devils. The smell of the sun had not left the earth, and little aimless winds blowing across the rose-gardens to the southward brought the scent of dried roses and water. Our fire once started, and the dogs craftily disposed to wait the dash of the porcupine, we climbed to the top of a rain-scarred hillock of earth, and looked across the scrub seamed with cattle-paths, white with the long grass, and dotted with spots of level pond-bottom, where the snipe would gather in winter.

"This," said Ortheris, with a sigh, as he

took in the unkempt desolation of it all, "this is sanguinary. This is unusual sanguinary. Sort o' mad country. Like a grate when the fire's put out by the sun." He shaded his eyes against the moonlight. "An' there's a loony dancin' in the middle of it all. Quite right. I'd dance too if I wasn't so downheart."

There pranced a portent in the face of the moon—a huge and ragged spirit of the waste, that flapped its wings from afar. It had risen out of the earth; it was coming toward us, and its outline was never twice the same. The toga, table-cloth, or dressing-gown, whatever the creature wore, took a hundred shapes. Once it stopped on a neighboring mound and flung all its legs and arms to the winds.

"My, but that scarecrow 'as got 'em bad!" said Ortheris. "Seems like if 'e comes any furder we'll 'ave to argify with 'im."

Learoyd raised himself from the dirt as a bull clears his flanks of the wallow. And as the bull bellows, so he, after a short minute at gaze, gave tongue to the stars.

"MULVAANEY! MULVAANEY! A hoo!"

Then we yelled all together, and the figure dipped into the hollow, till, with a crash of rending grass, the lost one strolled up to the light of the fire and disappeared to the waist in a wave of joyous dogs. Then Learoyd and Ortheris gave greeting, bass and falsetto

together, both swallowing a lump in the
throat.

" You damned fool !" said they, and sev-
erally pounded him with their fists.

" Go easy !" he answered, wrapping a huge
arm round each. " I would have you know
that I am a god, to be treated as such—tho,'
by me faith, I fancy I've got to go to the
guard-room just like a privit soldier."

The latter part of the sentence destroyed
the suspicions raised by the former. Any
one would have been justified in regarding
Mulvaney as mad. He was hatless and
shoeless, and his shirt and trowsers were
dropping off him. But he wore one won-
drous garment—a gigantic cloak that fell
from collar-bone to heel—of pale pink silk,
wrought all over in the cunningest needle-
work of hands long since dead, with the
loves of the Hindu gods. The monstrous
figures leaped in and out of the light of the
fire as he settled the folds round him.

Ortheris handled the stuff respectfully for
a moment while I was trying to remember
where I had seen it before. Then he
screamed, " What *'ave* you done with the
palanquin ? You're wearin' the linin'."

" I am," said the Irishman, " an' by the
same token the 'broidery is scrapin' me hide
off. I've lived in this sumpshus counter-
pane for four days. Me son, I begin to on-
dherstand why the naygur is no use. Widout me boots, an' me trousies like an open-

work stocking on a gyurl's leg at a dance, I begin to feel like a naygur-man—all fearful and timoreous. Give me a pipe an' I'll tell on.''

He lighted a pipe, resumed his grip of his two friends, and rocked to and fro in a gale of laughter.

"Mulvaney," said Ortheris, sternly, "'tain't no time for laughin'. You've given Jock an' me more trouble than you're worth. You 'ave been absent without leave, an' you'll go into cells for that; an' you've come back disgustin'ly dressed an' most improper in the linin' o' that bloomin' palanquin. Instid of which you laugh. An' *we* thought you was dead all the time."

"Bhoys," said the culprit, still shaking gently, "whin I've done me tale you may cry if you like, an' little Orth'ris here can thrample me inside out. Ha' done an' listen. Me performinces have been stupenjus; me luck has been the blessed luck av the British army—an' there's no better than that. I went out dhrunk an' drinkin' in the palanquin, an' I have come back a pink god. Did any av you go to Dearsley afther me time was up? He was at the bottom of ut all."

"Ah said so," murmured Learoyd. "To-morrow ah'll smash t'face in upon his heead."

"Ye will not. Dearsley's a jool av a man. Afther Ortheris had put me into the palanquin an' the six bearer-men were gruntin'

down the road, I tuk thought to mock Dearsley for that fight. So I tould thim, 'Go to
th' embankmint,' and there, bein' most
amazin' full, I shtuck me head out av the
concern, an' passed compliments wid Dearsley. I must ha' miscalled him outrageous,
for whin I am that way the power av the
tongue comes on me. I can bare remimber
tellin' him that his mouth opened endways
like the mouth av a skate, which was thrue
afther Learoyd had handled ut; an' I clear
remimber his takin' no manner nor matter
av offense, but givin' me a big dhrink av
beer. 'Twas the beer did the thrick, for I
crawled back into the palanquin, steppin'
on me right ear wid me left foot, and thin I
slept like the dead. Wanst I half roused,
an' begad the noise in me head was tremenjus—roarin' an' rattlin' an' poundin', such
as was quite new to me. ' Mother av Mercy,'
thinks I, 'fwhat a concertina I will have on
me shoulders whin I wake!' An' wid that
I curls mesilf up to sleep before ut should
get hould on me. Bhoys, that noise was not
dhrink, 'twas the rattle av a thrain !"

There followed an impressive pause.

"Yes, he had put me on a thrain—put me,
palanquin an' all, an' six black-assassins av
his own coolies that was in his nefarious
confidence, on the flat av a ballast-thruck,
and we were rowlin' on, bowlin' along to
Benares. Glory be that I did not wake up
thin an' introjuce mesilf to the coolies. As

I was sayin', I slept for the betther part av a day an' a night. But remimber you, that that man Dearsley had packed me off on wan av his material-thrains to Benares, all for to make me over-stay me leave an' get me into the cells."

The explanation was an eminently rational one. Benares was at least ten hours by rail from the cantonments, and nothing in the world could have saved Mulvaney from arrest as a deserter had he appeared there in the apparel of his orgies. Dearsley had not forgotten to take revenge. Learoyd, drawing back a little, began to place soft blows over selected portions of Mulvaney's body. His thoughts were away on the embankment, and they meditated evil for Dearsley. Mulvaney continued:

"Whin I was full awake the palanquin was set down in a street, I suspicioned, for I cud hear people passin' an' talkin'. But I knew well I was far from home. There is a queer smell upon our cantonments—smell av dried earth an' brick-kilns wid whiffs av a cavalry stable-litter. This place smelled marigold flowers an' bad water, an' wanst somethin' alive came an' blew heavy with his muzzle at the chink av the shutter. 'It's in a village I am,' thinks I to mesilf, 'an' the parochial buffalo is investigatin' the palanquin.' But any ways I had no desire to move. Only lie still whin you're in foreign parts an' the standin' luck av the British army will carry ye through. That is an epigram. I made ut.

"Thin a lot av whisperin' divils sur-rounded the palanquin. 'Take ut up,' says wan man. 'But who'll pay us?' says an-other. 'The Maharanee's minister, av coorse,' sez the man. 'Oho!' sez I to me-silf, 'I'm a quane in me own right, wid a minister to pay me expinses. I'll be an emperor if I lie still long enough. But this is no village I've struck.' I lay quiet, but I gummed me right eye to a crack av the shutters, an' I saw that the whole street was crammed wid palanquins an' horses an' a sprinklin' av naked priests, all yellow pow-der an' tigers' tails. But I may tell you, Orth'ris, an' you, Learoyd, that av all the palanquins ours was the most imperial an' magnificent. Now a palanquin means a na-tive lady all the world over, excipt whin a soldier av the quane happens to be takin' a ride. 'Women an' priests!' sez I. 'Your father's son is in the right pew this time, Terence. There will be proceedin's.' Six black divils in pink muslin tuk up the pa-lanquin, an' oh! but the rowlin' an' the rockin' made me sick. Thin we got fair jammed among the palanquins—not more than fifty av them—an' we grated an' bumped like Queenstown potato-smacks in a runnin' tide. I cud hear the women gig-glin' an' squirkin' in their palanquins, but mine was the royal equipage. They made

way for ut, an' begad, the pink muslin men
o' mine were howlin', ' Room for the Maharanee av Gokral-Seetarun.' Do you know
aught av the lady, sorr?"

"Yes," said I. "She is a very estimable
old queen of the Central Indian States, and
they say she is fat. How on earth could she
go to Benares without all the city knowing
her palanquin?"

" 'Twas the eternal foolishness av the nay-
gur-men. They saw the palanquin lyin'
loneful an' forlornsome, an' the beauty av
ut, after Dearsley's men had dhropped ut
an' gone away, an' they gave ut the best
name that occurred to thim. Quite right
too. For aught we know the ould lady was
thravelin' *incog.*—like me. I'm glad to hear
she's fat. I was no light weight mesilf, an'
me men were mortial anxious to dhrop me
under a great big archway promiscuously
ornamented with the most improper carv-
in's an' cuttin's I iver saw. Begad! they
made me blush—like a—like maharanee."

"The temple of Prithi-Devi," I murmured, remembering the monstrous horrors
of that sculptured archway at Benares.

"Pretty Devilskins, savin' your presence,
sorr. There was nothin' pretty about ut,
except me! 'Twas all half dhark, an' whin
the coolies left they shut a big black gate
behind av us, an' half a company av fat yellow priests began pullyhaulin' the palanquins into a dharker place yet—a big stone

hall full av pillars an' gods an' incense, an'
all manner of similar thruck. The gate dis-
concerted me, for I perceived I wud have to
go forward to get out, my retreat bein' cut
off. By the same token a good priest makes
a bad palanquin-coolie. Begad ! they nearly
turned me inside out draggin' the palanquin
to the temple. Now the disposishin av the
forces inside was this way. The Maharanee
av Gokral-Seetarun—that was me—lay by
the favor av Providence on the far left flank
behind the dhark av a pillar carved with
elephants's heads. The remainder av the
palanquins was in a big half circle facing in
to the biggest, fattest, an' most amazin' she-
god that iver I dreamed av. Her head ran up
into the black above us, an' her feet stuck
out in the light av a little fire av melted
butter that a priest was feedin' out av a but-
ter-dish. Thin a man began to sing an'
play on somethin' back in the dhark, an' 'twas
a queer song. Ut made me hair lift on the
back av me neck. Thin the doors av all
the palanquins slid back, an' the women
bundled out. I saw what I'll niver see agin.
'Twas more glorious than transformations at
a pantomime, for they was in pink an' blue
an' silver an' red an grass-green, wid di'-
monds an' imralds an' great red rubies all
over thim. But that was the least part av
the glory. Oh, bhoys, they were more lovely
than the like av any loveliness in Hivin ; ay,
their little bare feet were better than the

white hands av a lord's lady, an' their mouths were like puckered roses, an' their eyes were bigger an' dharker than the eyes av any livin' women I've seen. Ye may laugh, but I'm speakin' truth. I never saw the like, an' never I will again."

"Seeing that in all probablity you were watching the wives and daughters of most of the kings of India, the chances are that you won't," I said, for it was dawning on me that Mulvaney had stumbled upon a big queens' praying at Benares.

" I niver will," he said, mournfully. "That sight doesn't come twist to any man. It made me ashamed to watch. A fat priest knocked at me door. I did'nt think he'd have the insolince to disturb the Maharanee av Gokral-Seetarun, so I lay still. ' The old cow's asleep,' sez he to another. ' Let her be,' sez that. ' 'Twill be long before she has a calf!' I might ha' known before he spoke that all a woman prays for in Injia—an' for matter o' that in England, too—is childher. That made me more sorry I'd come, me bein', as you well know, a childless man."

He was silent for a moment, thinking of his little son, dead many years ago.

" They prayed, an' the butter-fires blazed up an' the incense turned everything blue, an' between that an' the fires the women looked as tho' they were all ablaze an' twinklin'. They tuk hold av the she-god's knees, they cried out an' they threw

thimsilves about, an' that world-without-
end-amen music was dhriving thim mad.
Mother av Hivin! how they cried, an' the
old she-god grinnin' above them all so
scornful! The dhrink was dyin' out in me
fast, an' I was thinkin' harder than the
thoughts wud go through me head—thinkin' how to get out an' all manner of nonsinse
as well. The women were rockin' in rows,
their di'mond belts clickin', an' the tears
runnin' out betune their hands, an' the
lights were goin' lower and dharker. Thin
there was a blaze like lightnin' from the
roof, an' that showed me the inside av the
palanquin, an' at the end where my foot was
stood the livin' spit an' image o' myself
worked on the linin'. This man here, it
was.''

He hunted in the folds of his pink cloak,
ran a hand under one, and thrust into the
fire-light a foot-long embroidered present-
ment of the great god Krishna, playing on
a flute. The heavy jowl, the staring eye, and
the blue-black mustache of the god made
up a far-off resemblance to Mulvaney.

"The blaze was gone in a wink, but the
whole schame came to me thin. I believe
I was mad, too. I slid the off shutter open
an' rowled out into the dhark behind the
elephint-head pillar, tucked up me trousies
to me knees, slipped off me boots an' tuk a
general hould av all the pink linin' av the
palanquin. Glory be, ut ripped out like a

woman's dhriss when you tread on ut at a serjint's ball, and a bottle came with ut. I
tuk the bottle an' the next minut I was out
av the dhark av the pillar, the pink linin'
wrapped round me most graceful, the music
thunderin' like kettle-drums, an' a cowld
draft blowin' round me bare legs. By this
hand that did ut, I was Krishna tootlin' on
the flute—the god that the rig'mintal chaplain talks about. A sweet sight I must ha'
looked. I knew me eyes were big, an' me
face was wax white, an' at the worst I must
ha' looked like a ghost. But they took me
for the livin' god. The music stopped, an'
the women were dead dumb, an' I crooked
me legs like a shepherd on a china basin,
an' I did the ghost-waggle with me feet as I
had done ut at the rig'mintal theatre many
times, an' I slid acrost the width av that
temple in front av the she god tootlin' on
the beer bottle."

"Wot did you toot?" demanded Ortheris
the practical.

"Me? Oh!" Mulvaney sprung up, suit-
ing the action to the word, and slidin'
gravely in front of us, a dilapidated but im-
posing deity in the half light. "I sung:

> "'Only say
> You'll be Mrs. Brallaghan,
> Don't say nay,
> Charmin' Judy Callaghan.'

I didn't know me own voice when I sung.

An' oh! 'twas pitiful to see the women.
The darlin's were down on their faces.
Whin I passed the last wan I cud see her
poor little fingers workin' one in another as
if she wanted to touch me feet. So I dhrew
the tail av this pink overcoat over her head
for the greater honor, an' I slid into the
dhark on the other side av the temple, an'
fetched up in the arms av a big fat priest.
All I wanted was to get away clear. So I
tuk him by his greasy throat an' shut the
speech out av him. 'Out!' sez I. 'Which
way, ye fat heathen?' 'Oh!' sez he. 'Man,'
sez I. 'White man, soldier man, common
soldier man. Where in the name av confusion is the back door?' The women in the
temple were still on their faces an' a young
priest was holdin' out his arms above their
heads.

"' This way,' sez me fat friend, duckin'
behind a big bull-god an' divin' into a passage. Thin I remimbered that I must ha'
made the miraculous reputation av that
temple for the next fifty years. 'Not so
fast,' I sez, an' I held out both me hands
wid a wink. That ould thief smiled like a
father. I tuk him by the back av the neck
in case he should be wishful to put a knife
into me unbeknownst, an' I ran him up an
down the passage twice to collect his sensi-
bilities! 'Be quiet!' sez he, in English.
'Now you talk sense,' I sez. 'Fwhat 'll you
give me for the use av that most iligant palan-

quin I have no time to take away?' 'Don't tell,' sez he. 'Is ut like?' sez I. 'But ye might give me me railway fare. I'm far from me home an' I've done you a service.' Bhoys 'tis a good thing to be a priest. The ould man niver throubled himself to dhraw from a bank. As I will prove to you subse-quint, he philandered all round the slack av his clothes an' began dribblin' ten-rupee notes, old gold mohurs, an' rupees into me hand till I could hould no more."

" You lie!" said Ortheris. " You're mad or sunstrook. A native don't give coin un-less you cut it out o' 'im. 'Tain't nature."

" Thin me lie an' me sunstroke is con-cealed under that lump av sod yonder," re-torted Mulvaney unruffled, nodding across the scrub. " An' there's a dale more in nat-ure than your squidgy little legs have iver taken you to, Orth'ris, me son. Four hun-dred and thirty-four rupees by me reckon-in', *an'* a big fat gold necklace that I took from him as a remimbrancer, was our share in that business."

" An' 'e give it you for love?" said Or-theris.

" We were alone in that passage. May be I was a trifle too pressin', but considher fwhat I had done for the good av the temple an' the iverlastin' joy av those women. 'Twas cheap at the price. I wud ha' taken more if I cud ha' found ut. I turned the ould man upside down at the last, but he

was milked dhry. Thin he opened a door
in another passage an' I found mysilf up to
me knees in Benares river-water, an' bad
smellin' ut is. More by token I had come
out on the river-line close to a cracklin'
corpse. This was in the heart av the night,
for I had been four hours in the temple.
There was a crowd av boats tied up, so I tuk
wan an' wint across the river. Thin I came
home acrost country, lyin' up by day."

"How on earth did you manage?" I said.

"How did Sir Frederick Roberts get from
Cabul to Candahar? He marched an' he
niver tould how near he was to breakin'
down. That's why he is fwhat he is. An'
now—" Mulvaney yawned portentously.
"Now I will go an' give mesilf up for ab-
since widout leave. It's eight-an'-twinty
days, an' the rough end of the colonel's
tongue in orderly-room any way you look
at ut. But 'tis cheap at the price."

"Mulvaney," said I, softly, "if there
happens to be any sort of excuse that the
colonel can in any way accept, I have a
notion that you'll get nothing more than
the dressing-down. The new recruits are in,
and—"

"Not a word more, sorr. Is ut excuses
the ould man wants? 'Tis not my way,
but he shall have thim. I'll tell him I was
engaged in financial operations connected
wid a church," and he flapped his way to
cantonments and the cells, singing lustily :

"So they sent a corp'ril's file,
    And they put me in the gyard-room
    For conduck unbecomin' of a soldier."

And when he was lost in the haze of the moonlight we could hear the refrain :

"Bang upon the big drum, bash upon the cymbals,
    As we go marchin' along, boys oh !
    For although in this campaign
    There's no whisky nor champagne,
    We'll keep our spirits goin with a song, boys !"

Therewith he surrendered himself to the joyful and almost weeping guard, and was made much of by his fellows. But to the colonel he said he had been smitten with sunstroke and had lain insensible on a villager's cot for untold hours, and between laughter and good will the affair was smoothed over, so that he could next day teach the new recruits how to "Fear God, Honor the Queen, Shoot Straight, and Keep Clean."

There is no further space to record the digging up of the spoils, or the triumphal visit of the three to Dearsley, who feared for his life, but was most royally treated instead, and under that influence told how the palanquin had come into his possession. But that is another story.

**12**

# THE COURTING OF DINAH SHADD.

## I.

ALL day I had followed at the heels of a pursuing army, engaged on one of the finest battles that ever camp of exercise beheld. Thirty thousand troops had by the wisdom of the government of India been turned loose over a few thousand square miles of country to practice in peace what they would never attempt in war. Consequently cavalry charged unshaken infantry at the trot; infantry captured artillery by frontal attacks, delivered in line of quarter columns; and mounted infantry skirmished up to the wheels of an armored train, which carried nothing more deadly than a twenty-five pounder Armstrong, two Nordenfeldts, and a few score volunteers, all cased in three-eighths-inch boiler-plate. Yet it was a very life-like camp. Operations did not cease at sundown; nobody knew the country, and nobody was to spare man or horse. There was unending cavalry scouting, and almost unending forced work over broken ground.

The Army of the South had finally pierced the centre of the Army of the North, and was pouring through the gap, hot foot, to capture a city of strategic importance. Its front extended fanwise, the sticks being represented by regiments strung out along the line of route backward to the divisional transport columns, and all the lumber that trails behind an army on the move. On its right the broken left of the Army of the North was flying in mass, chased by the Southern horse and hammered by the Southern guns, till these had been pushed far beyond the limits of their last support. Then the flying Army of the North sat down to rest, while the elated commandant of the pursuing force telegraphed that he held it in check and observation.

Unluckily he did not observe that three miles to his right flank a flying column of Northern horse, with a detachment of Ghoorkhas and British troops, had been pushed round as fast as the falling light allowed, to cut across the entire rear of the Southern Army, to break, as it were, all the ribs of the fan where they converged, by striking at the transport reserve, ammunition, and artillery supplies. Their instructions were to go in, avoiding a few scouts who might not have been drawn off by the pursuit, and create sufficient excitement to impress the Southern Army with the wisdom of guarding their own flank and rear before they captured cities. It was a pretty maneuver, neatly carried out.

Speaking for the second division of the Southern Army, our first intimation of it was at twilight, when the artillery were laboring in deep sand, most of the escort were trying to help them out, and the main body of the infantry had gone on. A Noah's ark of elephants, camels, and the mixed menagerie of an Indian transport train bubbled and squealed behind the guns, when there appeared from nowhere in particular British infantry to the extent of three companies, who sprung to the heads of the gun horses, and brought all to a stand-still amid oaths and cheers.

"How's that, umpire?" said the major commanding the attack, and with one voice the drivers and limber gunners answered, "Hout!" while the colonel of artillery sputtered.

"All your scouts are charging our main body," said the major. "Your flanks are unprotected for two miles. I think we've broken the back of this division. And listen! there go the Ghoorkhas!"

A weak fire broke from the rear guard more than a mile away, and was answered by cheerful howlings. The Ghoorkhas, who should have swung clear of the second division, had stepped on its tail in the dark, but, drawing off, hastened to reach the next line, which lay almost parallel to us, five or six miles away.

Our column swayed and surged irreso-

lutely—three batteries, the divisional ammunition reserve, the baggage, and a section
of hospital and bearer corps. The commandant ruefully promised to report himself "cut up" to the nearest umpire, and
commending his cavalry and all other cavalry to the care of Eblis, toiled on to resume
touch with the rest of the division.

"We'll bivouac here to-night," said the
major. "I have a notion that the Ghoorkhas will get caught. They may want us to
reform on. Stand easy till the transport
gets away."

A hand caught my beast's bridle and led
him out of the choking dust; a larger hand
deftly canted me out of the saddle, and two
of the hugest hands in the world received
me sliding. Pleasant is the lot of the special correspondent who falls into such hands
as those of Privates Mulvaney, Ortheris and
Learoyd.

"An' that's all right," said the Irishman,
calmly. "We thought we'd find you somewheres here by. Is there anything of yours
in the transport? Orth'ris 'll fetch ut out."

Ortheris did "fetch ut out" from under
the trunk of an elephant, in the shape of
a servant and an animal, both laden with
medical comforts. The little man's eyes
sparkled.

"If the brutil an' licentious soldiery av
these parts gets sight av the thruck," said
Mulvaney, making practiced investigation,

"they'il loot ev'rything. They're bein' fed on iron-filin's an' dog biscuit these days, but glory's no compensation for a bellyache. Praise be, we're here to protect you, sorr. Beer, sausage, bread (soft, an' that's a cur'-osity), soup in a tin; whisky by the smell av ut, an' fowls. Mother av Moses, but ye take the field like a confectioner! 'Tis scand'lus."

"'Ere's a orficer," said Ortheris, signifi-cantly. "When the sarjint's done lushin', the privit may clean the pot."

I bundled several things into Mulvaney's haversack before the major's hand fell on my shoulder, and he said, tenderly: "Requisi-tioned for the queen's service. Wolseley was quite wrong about special correspond-ents. They are the best friends of the sol-dier. Come an' take pot-luck with us to-night."

And so it happened amid laughter and shoutings that my well-considered commis-sariat melted away to reappear on the mess-table, which was a water-proof sheet spread on the ground. The flying column had taken three days' rations with it, and there be few things nastier than government rations—es-pecially when government is experimenting with German toys. Erbswurst, tinned beef, of surpassing tinniness, compressed vegeta-bles, and meat biscuits may be nourishing, but what Thomas Atkins wants is bulk in his inside. The major, assisted by his brother officers, purchased goats for the camp, and so made the experiment of no effect. Long before the fatigue-party sent to collect brushwood had returned the men were settled down by their valises, kettles and pots had appeared from the surrounding country, and were dangling over fires as the kid and the compressed vegetables bubbled together; then a cheerful clinking of mess tins, outrageous demands for " a little more stuffin'" with that there liver wing," and gust on gust of chaff as pointed as a bayonet and as delicate as a gun-butt.

" The boys are in good temper," said the major. " They'll be singing presently. Well, a night like this is enough to keep them happy."

Over our heads burned the wonderful Indian stars, which are not all pricked in on one plane, but preserving an orderly perspective, draw the eye through the velvet darkness of the void up to the barred doors of heaven itself. The earth was a gray shadow more unreal than the sky. We could hear her breathing lightly in the pauses between the howling of the jackals, the movement of the wind in the tamarisks, and the fitful mutter of musketry-fire leagues away to the left. A native woman in some unseen hut began to sing, the mail train thundered past on its way to Delhi, and a roosting crow cawed drowsily. Then there was a belt-loosening silence about the fires, and the even breathing of the crowded earth took up the story.

The men, full fed, turned to tobacco and song—their officers with them. Happy is the subaltern who can win the approval of the musical critics in his regiment, and is honored among the more intricate step dancers. By him, as by him who plays cricket craftily, will Thomas Atkins stand in time of need when he will let a better officer go on alone. The ruined tombs of forgotten Mussulman saints heard the ballad of "Agra Town," "The Buffalo Battery," "Marching to Kabul," "The Long, Long Indian Day," "The Place Where the Punka Coolie Died," and that crashing chorus which announces

> " Youth's daring spirit, manhood's fire,
>     Firm hand and eagle eye
> Must he acquire who would aspire
>     To see the gray boar die."

To-day, of all those jovial thieves who appropriated my commissariat, and lay and laughed round that water-proof sheet, not one remains. They went to camps that were not of exercise and battles without umpires. Burma, the Soudan, and the frontier fever and fight took them in their time.

I drifted across to the men's fires in search of Mulvaney, whom I found strategically greasing his feet by the blaze. There is nothing particularly lovely in the sight of a private thus engaged after a long day's march, but when you reflect on the exact portion of the " might, majesty, dominion, and power" of the British Empire that stands on those feet, you take an interest in the proceedings.

" There's a blister—bad luck to ut!—on me heel," said Mulvaney. " I can't touch it. Prick ut out, little man."

Ortheris produced his housewife, eased the trouble with a needle, stabbed Mulvaney in the calf with the same weapon, and was incontinently kicked into the fire.

" I've bruk the best av me toes over you, ye grinnin' child av disruption!" said Mulvaney, sitting cross-legged and nursing his feet; then, seeing me : "Oh, ut's you, sorr ! Be welkim, an' take that maraudin scutts' place. Jock, hold him down on the cindhers for a bit."

But Ortheris escaped and went elsewhere as I took possession of the hollow he had scraped for himself and lined with his great-coat. Learoyd, on the other side of the fire, grinned affably, and in a minute fell asleep.

" There's the height av politeness for you," said Mulvaney, lighting his pipe with a flaming branch. " But Jock's eaten half a box av your sardines at wan gulp, an' I think the tin too. What's the best wid you, sorr ; an' how did you happen to be

on the losin' side this day when we captured you?"

"The Army of the South is winning all
along the line," I said.

"Then that line's the hangman's rope,
savin' your presence. You'll learn to-morrow how we rethreated to dhraw thim on
before we made thim trouble, an' that's what
a woman does. By the same tokin, we'll be
attacked before the dawnin', an' ut would
be betther not to slip your boots. How do
I know that? By the light av pure reason.
Here are three companies av us ever so far
inside av the enemy's flank, an' a crowd av
roarin', t'arin', an' squealin' cavalry gone on
just to turn out the whole nest av thim.
Av course the enemy will pursue by bri-
gades like as not, an' then we'll have to run
for ut. Mark me words. I am av the opinion av Polonius whin he said : ' Don't fight
wid ivry scutt for the pure joy av fightin';
but if you do, knock the nose av him first
an' frequint!' We ought to ha' gone on an'
helped the Ghoorkhas."

"But what do you know about Polonius?" I demanded. This was a new side
of Mulvaney's character.

"All that Shakespeare ever wrote, an' a
dale more than the gallery shouted," said
the man of war, carefully lacing his boots.
"Did I not tell you av Silver's Theatre in
Dublin whin I was younger than I am now
an' a patron av the drama? Ould Silver

wud never pay actor, man or woman, their just dues, an' by consequence his comp'-nies was collapsible at the last minut'. Then the bhoys would clamor to take a part, an' oft as not ould Silver made thim pay for the fun. Faith, I've seen Hamlut played wid a new black eye, an' the queen as full as a cornucopia. I remember wanst Hogin, that 'listed in the Black Tyrone an' was shot in South Africa, he sejuced ould Silver into givin' him Hamlut's part instid av me, that had a fine fancy for rhetoric in those days. Av course I wint into the gallery an' began to fill the pit wid other people's hats, an' I passed the time av day to Hogin walk-in' through Denmark like a hamstrung mule wid a pall on his back. 'Hamlut,' sez I, 'there's a hole in your heel. Pull up your shtockins Hamlut,' sez I. 'Hamlut, Ham-lut, for the luv av decincy dhrop that skull and pull up your shtockins.' The whole house begun to tell him that. He stopped his soliloquishms mid between. 'My shtock-ins may be comin' down or they may not,' sez he, screwin' his eye into the gallery, for well he knew who I was; 'but afther the performince is over me an' the Ghost 'll trample the guts out av you, Terence, wid your ass's bray.' An' that's how I come to know about Hamlut. Eyah! Those days, those days! Did you iver have onendin' developmint an' nothin' to pay for it in your life, sor?"

" Never without having to pay," I said.

" That's thrue. 'Tis mane, whin you considher on ut; but ut's the same wid horse
or fut. A headache if you dhrink, an' a
bellyache if you eat too much, an' a heart-
ache to kape it all down. Faith, the beast
only gets the colic, an' he's the lucky man."

He dropped his head and stared into the
fire, fingering his mustache the while. From
the far side of the bivouac the voice of Cor-
bet-Nolan, senior subaltern of B Company,
uplifted itself in an ancient and much-ap-
preciated song of sentiment, the men moan-
ing melodiously behind him:

'' The north wind blew coldly, she drooped from that
 hour,
 My own little Kathleen, my sweet little Kathleen,
 Kathleen, my Kathleen, Kathleen O'Moore!"

with forty-five *o's* in the last word. Even at
that distance you might have cut the soft
South Irish accent with a shovel.

" For all we take we must pay; but the
price is cruel high," murmured Mulvaney
when the chorus had ceased.

" What's the trouble?" I said, gently, for
I knew that he was a man of an inextin-
guishable sorrow.

" Hear now," said he. " Ye know what
I am now. I know what I mint to be at the
beginnin' av me service. I've tould you
time an' again, an' what I have not, Dinah

Shadd has. An' what am I? Oh, Mary,
Mother av Eivin! an ould dhrunken, un-
trustable baste av a privit that has seen the
rig'mint change out from colonel to drummer-boy, not wanst er twicet, but scores av
times! Ay, scores! An' me not so near
gettin' promotion as in the furst. An' me
livin' on an' kapin' clear o' Clink not by me
own good conduck, but by the kindness av
some orficer—bhoy young enough to be son
to me! Do I not know ut? Can I not tell
whin I'm passed over at p'rade, tho' I'm
rockin' full av liquor an' ready to fall all in
wan piece, such as even a suckin' child
might see, bekaze, ' Oh, 'tis only ould Mulvaney !' An' whin I'm let off in the ord'ly-
room, through some thrick av the tongue
an' a ready answer an'the ould man's mercy,
is ut smilin' I feel whin I fall away an' go
back to Dinah Shadd, thryin' to carry ut all
off as a joke? Not I. 'Tis hell to me—
dumb hell through ut all; an' the next time
whin the fit comes I will be as bad again.
Good cause the rig'mint has to know me
for the best soldier in ut. Better cause have
I to know mesilf for the worst man. I'm
only fit to tache the new drafts what I'll
never learn mesilf; an' I am sure as tho' I
heard ut, that the minut wan av these pink-
eyed recruits gets away from me ' Mind ye,
now,' an' ' Listen to this, Jim, bhoy,' sure
I am that the serjint houlds me up to him
for a warnin'. So I tache, as they say at

musketry instruction, by direct an' ricochet fire. Lord be good to me! for I have stud some trouble."

"Lie down and go to sleep," said I, not being able to comfort or advise. "You're the best man in the regiment, and, next to Ortheris, the biggest fool. Lie down, and wait till we're attacked. What force will they turn out? Guns, think you?"

"Thry that wid your lorrds, an' ladies, twistin' an' turnin' the talk, tho' you mint ut well. Ye cud say nothin' to help me; an' yet ye niver knew what cause I had to be what I am."

"Begin at the beginning and go on to the end," I said, royally. "But rake up the fire a bit first." I passed Ortheris's bayonet for a poker.

"That shows how little you know what to do," said Mulvaney, putting it aside. "Fire takes all the heart out av the steel, an' the next time, may be, that our little man is fightin' for his life his brad-awl 'll break, an' so you'll 'ave killed him, manin' no more than to kape yourself warm. 'Tis a recruitie's thrick that. Pass the cl'anin'-rod, sorr."

I snuggled down, abashed, and after an interval the low, even voice of Mulvaney began.

## II.

"Did I ever tell you how Dinah Shadd came to be wife av mine?"

I dissembled a burning anxiety that I had felt for some months—ever since Dinah Shadd, the strong, the patient, and the infinitely tender, had, of her own good love and free-will, washed a shirt for me, moving in a barren land where washing was not.

"I can't remember," I said, casually. "Was it before or after you made love to Annie Bragin, and got no satisfaction?"

The story of Annie Bragin is written in another place. It is one of the many episodes in Mulvaney's checkered career.

"Before—before—long before was that business av Annie Bragin an' the corp'ril's ghost. Never woman was the worse for me whin I had married Dinah. There's a time for all things, an' I know how to kape all things in place—barrin' the dhrink, that kapes me in me place, wid no hope av comin' to be aught else."

"Begin at the beginning," I insisted. "Mrs Mulvaney told me that you married her when you were quartered in Krab Bokhar barracks."

"An' the same is a cess-pit," said Mulvaney, piously. "She spoke thrue, did Dinah. 'Twas this way. Talkin' av that, have ye iver fallen in love, sorr?"

I preserved the silence of the damned. Mulvaney continued:

"Thin I will assume that ye have not. *I* did. In the days av me youth, as I have more than wanst tould you, I was a man

that filled the eye an' delighted the sowl av
women. Niver man was hated as I have
been. Niver man was loved as I—no, not
within half a day's march av ut. For
the first five years av me service, when I
was what I wud give me sowl to be now, I
tuk whatever was within me reach an' digested ut, an' that's more than most men
can say. Dhrink I tuk, an' ut did me no
harm. By the hollow av hivin, I could play
wid four women at wanst, an' kape them
from findin' out anything about the other
three, an' smile like a full-blown marigold
through ut all. Dick Coulhan, of the battery
we'll have down on us to-night, could dhrive
his team no better than I mine; an' I hild
the worse cattle. An' so I lived an' so I
was happy, till afther that business wid
Annie Bragin—she that turned me off as
cool as a meat-safe, an' taught where I stud
in the mind av an honest woman. 'Twas no
sweet dose to take.

" Afther that I sickened awhile, an' tuk
thought to me rig'mintal work, conceiting
mesilf I would study an' be a sarjint an' a
major-jineral twinty minutes afther that. But
on top o' me ambitiousness there was an'
empty place in me sowl, an' me own opinion
av mesilf cud not fill ut. Sez I to mesilf :
' Terence, you're a great man an' the best set
up in the rig'mint. Go on an' get promotion.'
Sez mesilf to me, ' What for ?' Sez I to mesilf, ' For the glory av ut.' Sez mesilf to me,

'Will that fill these two strong arrums av yours, Terence?' 'Go to the divil,' sez I to mesilf. 'Go to the married lines,' sez mesilf to me. ''Tis the same thing,' sez I to mesilf. 'Av you're the same man, ut is,' sez mesilf to me. An' wid that I considhered on ut a long while. Did you iver feel that way, sorr?"

I snored gently, knowing that if Mulvaney were uninterrupted he would go on. The clamor from the bivouac fires beat up to the stars as the rival singers of the companies were pitted against each other.

"So, I felt that way, an' bad time ut was. Wanst, bein' a fool, I went into the married lines, more for the sake av spakin' to our ould color-sarjint Shadd than for any thruck wid wimmen-folk. I was a corp'ril then— rejuced aftherwards; but a corp'ril then. I've got a photograft av mesilf to prove ut. 'You'll take a cup av tay wid us?' sez he. 'I will that,' I sez; 'tho' tay is not me divarsion.' ''Twud be better for you if ut were,' sez ould Mother Shadd. An' she had ought to know, for Shadd, in the ind av his service, dhrank bung-full each night.

" Wid that I tuk off me gloves—there was pipe-clay in thim so that they stud alone— an' pulled up me chair, lookin' at the china ornamints an' bits av things in the Shadds' quarters. They were things that belonged to a woman, an' no camp kit, here to-day an' dishipated next. 'You're comfortable in this place, serjint,' sez I. ' 'Tis the wife that did ut, boy,' sez he, pointin' the stem av his pipe to ould Mother Shadd, an' she smacked the top av his bald head upon the compliment. 'That manes you want money,' sez she.

"An' thin—an' thin whin the kettle was to be filled, Dinah came in—my Dinah— her sleeves rowled up to the elbow, an' her hair in a gowlden glory over her forehead, the big blue eyes beneath twinklin' like stars on a frosty night, an' the tread of her two feet lighter than waste paper from the colonel's basket in ord'ly-room when ut's emptied. Bein' but a shlip av a girl, she went pink at seein' me, an' I twisted me mustache an' looked at a picture forninst the wall. Never show a woman that ye care the snap av a finger for her, an' begad she'll come bleatin' to your boot-heels."

"I suppose that's why you followed Annie Bragin till everybody in the married quarters laughed at you," said I, remembering that unhallowed wooing, and casting off the disguise of drowsiness.

"I'm layin' down the gin'ral theory av the attack," said Mulvaney, driving his foot into the dying fire. "If you read the 'Soldier's Pocket-Book,' which never any soldier reads, you'll see that there are exceptions. When Dinah was out av the door (an' 'twas as tho' the sunlight had gone too), 'Mother av Hiven, serjint!' sez I, 'but is that your daughter?' 'I've believed that way these eighteen years,' sez ould Shadd, his eyes twinklin'. 'But Mrs. Shadd has her own opinion, like ivry other woman.' ''Tis wid yours this time, for a mericle,' sez Mother Shadd. 'Then why, in the name av fortune, did I never see her before?' sez I. 'Bekase you've been thraipsin' round wid the married women these three years past. She was a bit av a child till last year, an' she shot up wid the spring,' sez ould Mother Shadd. 'I'll thraipse no more,' sez I. 'D'ye mane that?' sez ould Mother Shadd, lookin' at me sideways, like a hen looks at a hawk whin the chickens are runnin' free. 'Thry me, an' tell,' sez I. Wid that I pulled on me gloves, dhrank off the tea, an' wint out av the house as stiff as at gin'ral p'rade, for well I knew that Dinah Shadd's eyes were in the small av me back out av the scullery window. Faith, that was the only time I mourned I was not a cav'lryman, for the sake av the spurs to jingle.

"I wint out to think, an' I did a powerful lot av thinkin', but ut all came round to that shlip av a girl in the dotted blue dhress, wid the blue eyes an' the sparkil in them. Thin I kept off canteen, an' I kept to the married quarthers or near by on the chanst av meetin' Dinah. Did I meet her? Oh, me time past wid a lump in me throat as big as me valise, an' me heart goin' like a

farrier's forge on a Saturday mornin'!
'Twas 'Good-day to ye, Miss Dinah,' an'
'Good-day t'you, corp'ril,' for a week or
two, an' divil a bit further could I get, bekaze av the respict I had to that girl that I
cud ha' broken betune finger an' thumb."

Here I giggled as I recalled the gigantic
figure of Dinah Shadd when she handed me
my shirt.

"Ye may laugh," grunted Mulvaney.
"But I'm speakin' the trut', an' 'tis you that
are in fault.　Dinah was a girl that wud ha'
taken the imperiousness out av the Duchess
av Clonmel in those days.　Flower hand,
foot av shod air, an' the eyes av the mornin'
she had.　That is me wife to-day—ould
Dinah, an' never aught else than Dinah
Shadd to me.

"'Twas after three weeks standin off an'
niver makin' headway excipt through the
eyes, that a little drummer-boy grinned in
me face whin I had admonished him wid
the buckle av me belt for riotin' all over the
place.　'An' I'm not the only wan that
doesn't kape to the barricks,' sez he.　I tuk
him by the scruff av his neck—me heart
was hung on a hair-thrigger those days, you
will understand—an', 'Out wid ut,' sez I,
'or I'll lave no bone av you unbruk.'
'Speak to Dempsey,' sez he, howlin'.
'Dempsey which?' sez I, 'ye unwashed
limb av Satan.'　'Of the Bobtailed Dhra-
goons,' sez he.　'He's seen her home from

her aunt's house in the civil lines four times this fortnight.' 'Child,' sez I, dhroppin' him, 'your tongue's stronger than your body. Go to your quarters. I'm sorry I dhressed you down.'

"At that I went four days to wanst huntin' Dempsey. I was mad to think that wid all me airs among women I shud ha' been ch'ated by a basin-faced fool av a cav'lryman not fit to trust on a mule thrunk. Presintly I found him in our lines—the Bobtails was quartered next us—an' a tallowy, top-heavy son av a she mule he was, wid his big brass spurs an' his plastrons on his epigastons an' all. But he niver flinched a hair.

"'A word wid you, Dempsey,' sez I. 'You've walked wid Dinah Shadd four times this fortnight gone.'

"'What's that to you?' sez he. 'I'll walk forty times more, an' forty on top av that, ye shovel-futted, clod-breakin' infantry lance-corp'ril.'

"Before I could gyard he had his gloved fist home on me cheek, an' down I went full sprawl. 'Will that contint you?' sez he, blowin' on his knuckles for all the world like a Scots Grays orf'cer. 'Contint?' sez I. 'For your own sake, man, take off your spurs, peel your jackut, an' onglove. 'Tis the beginnin' av the overture. Stand up!'

"He stud all he knew, but he niver peeled his jackut, an' his shoulders had no fair

play. I was fightin' for Dinah Shadd an'
that cut on me cheek. What hope had he
forninst me? 'Stand up!' sez I, time an'
again, when he was beginnin' to quarter the
ground an' gyard high an' go large. 'This
isn't riding-school,' sez I. 'Oh, man, stand
up, an' let me get at ye!' But whin I saw
he wud be runnin' about, I grup his shtock
in me left an' his waist-belt in me right an'
swung him clear to me right front, head
undher, he hammerin' me nose till the wind
was knocked out av him on the bare ground.
'Stand up,' sez I, 'or I'll kick your head
into your chist.' An' I wud ha' done ut,
too, so ragin' mad I was.

"'Me collar-bone's bruk,' sez he. 'Help
me back to lines. I'll walk wid her no
more.' So I helped him back.''

"And was his collar-bone broken?" I
asked, for I fancied that only Learoyd could
neatly accomplish that terrible throw.

"He pitched on his left shoulder-point.
It was. Next day the news was in both
barricks; an' whin I met Dinah Shadd wid
a cheek like all the rig'mintal tailors' sam-
ples, there was no 'Good-mornin', corp'ril,'
or aught else. 'An' what have I done, Miss
Shadd,' sez I, very bould, plantin' mesilf
forninst her, 'that ye should not pass the
time of day?'

"'Ye've half killed rough-rider Dempsey,' sez she, her dear blue eyes fillin' up.

"'May be,' sez I. 'Was he a friend av

yours that saw you home four times in a fortnight ?'

" ' Yes,' sez she, very bould ; but her mouth was down at the corners. 'An'— an' what's that to you?'

" ' Ask Dempsey,' sez I, purtendin' t go away.

" ' Did you fight for me then, ye silly man ?' she sez, tho' she knew ut all along.

" ' Who else ?' sez I ; an' I tuk one pace to the front.

" ' I wasn't worth ut,' sez she, fingerin' her apron.

" ' That's for me to say,' sez I. ' Shall I say ut ?'

" ' Yes,' sez she, in a saint's whisper; an' at that I explained mesilf ; an' she tould me that ivry man that is a man, an' many that is a woman, hears wanst in his life.

" ' But what made ye cry at startin', Dinah darlin' ?' sez I.

" ' Your—your bloody cheek,' sez she, duckin' her little head down on me sash (I was duty for the day), an' whimperin' like a sorrowful angel.

" Now a man cud take that two ways. I tuk ut as pleased me best, an' my first kiss wid ut. Mother av Innocence! but I kissed her on the tip av the nose an' undher the eye, an' a girl that let's a kiss come tumble- ways like that has never been kissed before. Take note av that, sorr. Thin we wint, hand in hand, to ould Mother Shadd like

two little childher, an' she said it was no bad
thing; an' ould Shadd nodded behind his
pipe, an' Dinah ran away to her own room.
That day I throd on rollin' clouds. All
earth was too small to hould me. Begad, I
cud ha' picked the sun out av the sky for a
live coal to me pipe, so magnificent I was.
But I tuk recruities at squad drill, an' began
with general battalion advance whin I shud
ha' been balance-steppin' 'em. Eyah! that
day! that day!''

A very long pause. " Well ?" said I.

" It was all wrong," said Mulvaney, with
an enormous sigh. " An' sure I know that
ev'ry bit av ut was me own foolishness.
That night I tuk maybe the half av three
pints—not enough to turn the hair av a man
in his natural sinses. But I was more than
half dhrunk wid pure joy, an' that canteen
beer was so much whisky to me. I can't
tell how ut came about, but *bekase* I had no
thought for any wan except Dinah, *bekase* I
hadn't slipped her little white arms from
me neck five minutes, *bekase* the breath av
her kiss was not gone from me mouth, I
must go through the married lines on me
way to quarthers, an' I must stay talkin' to
a red-headed Mullengar heifer av a girl, Judy
Sheehy, that was daughter to Mother
Sheehy, the wife av Nick Sheehy, the canteen serjint—the black curse av Shielygh be
on the whole brood that are above groun'
this day!

" ' An' what are ye houldin' your head that high for, corp'ril,' sez Judy. ' Come in an' thry a cup av tay,' she sez, standin' in the doorway.

" Bein' an onbustable fool, an' thinkin' av anythin' but tay, I wint.

" ' Mother's at canteen,' sez Judy, smoothin' the hair av hers that was like red snakes, an' lookin' at me corner-ways out av her green cat's eyes. 'Ye will not mind, corp'ril?'

" ' I can endure,' sez I. ' Ould Mother Sheehy bein' no diversion av mine, nor her daughter too.' Judy fetched the tay-things an' put thim on the table, leanin' over me very close to get them square. I dhrew back, thinkin' of Dinah.

" ' Is ut afraid you are av a girl alone?' sez Judy.

" ' No,' sez I. ' Why should I be?'

" ' That rests wid the girl,' sez Judy, dhrawin' her chair next to mine.

" ' Thin there let ut rest,' sez I ; an' thinkin' I'd been a trifle onpolite, I sez, ' The tay's not quite sweet enough for me taste. Put your little finger in the cup, Judy ; 'twill make ut necthar.'

" ' What's necthar?' sez she.

" ' Somethin' very sweet,' sez I ; an' for the sinful life av me I cud not help lookin' at her out av the corner av me eye, as I was used to look at a woman.

" ' Go on wid ye, corp'ril,' sez she. ' You're a flirt.'

" ' On me sowl I'm not,' sez I.

" ' Then you're a cruel handsome man, an' that's worse,' sez she, heavin' big sighs an' lookin' crossways.

" ' You know your own mind,' sez I.

" ' 'Twud be better for me if I did not,' sez she.

" ' There's a dale to be said on both sides av that,' sez I, unthinkin'.

" ' Say your own part av that, then, Terence darlin',' sez she; ' for begad I'm thinkin' I've said too much or too little for an honest girl;' an' wid that she put her arms round me neck an' kissed me.

" ' There's no more to be said after that,' sez I, kissin' her back again.   Oh, the mane scut that I was, me head ringin' wid Dinah Shadd!  How does ut come about, sorr, that whin a man has put the comether on wan woman he's sure bound to put ut on another?  'Tis the same thing at musketry. Wan day ev'ry shot goes wide or into the bank, an' the next—lay high, lay low, sight or snap—ye can't get off the bull's-eye for ten shots runnin'."

" That only happens to a man who has had a good deal of experience; he does it without thinking," I replied.

" Thankin' you for the compliment, sorr, ut may be so; but I'm doubtin' whether you mint ut for a compliment.  Hear now.  I sat there wid Judy on me knee, tellin' me all manner av nonsinse, an' sayin' ' yes ' an'

' no,' when I'd much better ha' kept tongue betune teeth. An' that was not an hour afther I had left Dinah. What I was thinkin' av I can not say.

"Prisently, quiet as a cat, ould Mother Sheehy came in velvet-dhrunk. She had her daughter's red-hair, but 'twas bald in patches, an' I cud see in her wicked ould face, clear as lightnin', what Judy wud be twenty year to come. I was for jumpin' up, but Judy niver moved.

"'Terence has promust, mother,' sez she, an' the cowld sweat bruk out all over me.

"Ould Mother Sheehy sat down of a heap, an' began playin' wid the cups. 'Thin you're a well-matched pair,' she sez very thick; 'for he's the biggest rogue that iver spoiled the queen's shoe-leather, an'—'

"'I'm off, Judy,' sez I. 'You should not talk nonsinse to your mother. Get her to bed, girl.'

"'Nonsinse?' sez the ould woman, prickin' up her ears like a cat, an' grippin' the table-edge. 'Twill be the most nonsinsical nonsinse for you, ye grinnin' badger, if nonsinse 'tis. Git clear, you. I'm goin' to bed.'

"I ran out into the dhark, me head in a stew' an' me heart sick, but I had sinse enough to see that I'd brought ut all on mesilf. 'It's this to pass the time av day to a panjandhrum of hell-cats,' sez I. 'What I've said an' what I've not said do not

matther.  Judy an' her dam will hould me
for a promust man, an' Dinah will give me
the go, an' I desarve ut.  I will go an' get
dhrunk,' sez I, 'an' forgit about ut, for 'tis
plain I'm not a marryin' man.'

"On me way to canteen I ran against
Lascelles, color-sarjint that was, av E Com-
p'ny—a hard, hard man, wid a tormint av a
wife.  'You've the head av a drowned man
on your shoulders,' sez he, 'an' you're goin'
where you'll get a worse wan.  Come back,'
sez he.  'Let me go,' sez I.  'I've thrown
me luk over the wall wid me own hand.
'Then that's not the way to get ut back
again,' sez he.  'Have out wid your throuble, ye fool-bhoy.'  An' I tould him how the
matther was.

"He sucked in his lower lip.  'You've
been thrapped,' sez he.  'Ju Sheedy wud be
the betther for a man's name to hers as soon
as she can.  An' ye thought ye'd put the
comether on her.  That's the naturil vanity
av the baste.  Terence, you're a big born
fool, but you're not bad enough to marry
into that comp'ny.  If you said anythin,'
an' for all your protestations I'm sure you
did—or did not, which is worse—eat ut all.
Lie like the father av all lies, but come out
of ut free av Judy.  Do I not know what ut
is to marry a woman that was the very spit
av Judy when she was young?  I'm gettin'
ould, and I've larnt patience; but you, Terence, you'd raise hand on Judy an' kill her

in a year. Never mind if Dinah gives you
the go; you desarved ut. Never mind if the
whole rig'mint laughs at you all day. Get
shut av Judy an' her mother. They can't
dhrag you to church, but if they do, they'll
dhrag you to hell. Go back to your quarthers an' lie down,' sez he. Thin, over his
shoulder, 'You *must* ha' done with thim.'

"Nixt day I wint to see Dinah; but there
was no tucker in me as I walked. I knew
the throuble wud come soon enough widout any handlin' av mine, an' I dreaded ut
sore.

"I heard Judy callin' me, but I hild
straight on to the Shadds' quarthers, an'
Dinah wud ha' kissed me, but I hild her
back.

"'Whin all's said, darlin',' sez I, 'you can
give ut me if you will, tho' I misdoubt 'twill
be so easy to come by thin.'

"I had scarce begun to put the explanation into shape before Judy and her mother
came to the door. I think there was a veranda, but I'm forgettin'.

"'Will ye not step in?' sez Dinah, pretty
an' polite, tho' the Shadds had no dealin's
with the Sheehys. Old Mother Shadd
looked up quick, and she was the fust to see
the throuble, for Dinah was her daughter.

"'I'm pressed for time to-day,' sez Judy,
as bould as brass; 'an' I've only come for
Terence, my promust man. 'Tis strange to
find him here the day afther the day.'

" Dinah looked at me as though I had hit her, an' I answered straight.

"' There was some nonsinse last night at the Sheehys' quarthers, an' Judy's carryin' on the joke, darlin',' sez I.

"' At the Sheehys' quarthers?' sez Dinah, very slow ; an' Judy cut in wid :

"' He was there from nine till tin, Dinah Shadd, an' the betther half av that time I was sittin' on his knee, Dinah Shadd. Ye may look an' ye may look an' ye may look me up an' down, but ye won't look away that Terence is me promust man. Terence darlin', 'tis time for us to be comin' home.'

" Dinah Shadd never said word to Judy. ' Ye left me at half-past eight,' she sez to me, ' an' I niver thought that ye'd leave me for Judy, promises or no promises. Go back wid her, you that have to be fetched by a girl! I'm done wid you,' sez she ; an' she ran into her own room, her mother followin'. So I was alone with those two women, an' at liberty to spake me sintiments.

"' Judy Sheehy,' sez I, 'if you made a fool av me betune the lights you shall not do ut in the day. I never promised you words or lines.'

"' You lie,' sez ould Mother Sheehy ; ' an' may ut choke you where you stand !' She was far gone in dhrink.

"' An' tho' ut choked me where I stud I'd not change,' sez I. ' Go home, Judy. I take shame for a dacint girl like you dhraggin' your mother out bareheaded on this errand. Here, now, an' have ut for an answer. I gave me word to Dinah Shadd yesterday, an' more blame to me I was with you last night talkin' nonsinse, but nothin' more. You've chosen to thry to hould me on ut. I will not be held thereby for anythin' in the world. Is that enough?'

"Judy wint pink all over. 'An' I wish you joy av the perjury,' sez she. 'You've lost a woman that would ha' wore her hand to the bone for your pleasure; an' 'deed, Terence, ye were not thrapped. . . .' Lascelles must ha' spoken plain to her. 'I am such as Dinah is—'deed I am! Ye've lost a fool av a girl that 'll never look at you again, an' ye've lost what ye niver had—your common honesty. If you manage your men as you manage your love-makin', small wonder they call you the worst corp'ril in the comp'ny. Come away, mother,' sez she.

"But divil a fut would the ould woman budge! 'D'you hould by that?' sez she, peerin' up under her thick gray eyebrows.

"'Ay, an' wud,' said I, tho' Dinah gave me the go twinty times. 'I'll have no thruck with you or yours,' sez I. 'Take your child away, ye shameless woman.'

"'An' am I shameless?' sez she, bringin' her hands up above her head. 'Thin what are you, ye lyin', schamin', week-kneed, dhirty-souled son of a sutler? Am *I* shameless? Who put the open shame on me an' me child that we shud go beggin' through the lines in daylight for the broken word of a man? Double portion of me shame be upon you, Terence Mulvaney, that think yersilf so strong! By Mary an' the saints, by blood an' water, an' by ivry sorrow that came into the world since the beginnin', the black blight fall on you an' yours, so that ye may niver be free from pain for another when ut's not your own! May your heart bleed in your breast drop by drop wid all your friends laughin' at the bleedin'! Strong you think yourself? May your strength be a curse to you to dhrive you into the divil's hands against your own will! Clear-eyed you are? May your eyes see clear ivry step av the dark path you take till the hot cinders av hell put thim out! May the ragin' dry thirst in me own ould bones go to you that you shall never pass bottle full nor glass empty! God preserve the light av your onderstandin' to you, me jewel av a bhoy, that ye may niver forget what you mint to be an' do, when you're wallowin' in the muck! May ye see the betther an' follow the worse as long as there's breath in your body! an' may ye die quick in a strange land watchin' your death before ut takes you an' onable to stir hand or foot!'

"I heard a scufflin' in the room behind, an' thin Dinah Shadd's hand dhropped into mine like a rose-leaf into a muddy road.

"'The half av that I'll take,' sez she, 'an' more too, if I can. Go home, ye silly-talkin' woman—go home an' confess.'

"'Come away! Come away!' sez Judy, pullin' her mother by the shawl. ''Twas none av Terence's fault. For the love av Mary stop the talkin'!'

"'An' you!' said ould Mother Sheehy, spinnin' round forninst Dinah. 'Will ye take the half av that man's load? Stand off from him, Dinah Shadd, before he takes you down too—you that look to be a quarthermaster-serjint's wife in five years. Ye look too high, child. Ye shall wash for the quarthermaster-sarjint, whin he pl'ases to give you the job out av charity; but a privit's wife ye shall be to the end, an' ivry sorrow of a privit's wife ye shall know, an' niver a joy but wan, that shall go from you like the tide from a rock. The pain of bearin' ye shall know, but niver the pleasure of givin' the breast; an' you shall put away a man-child into the common ground wid niver a priest to say a prayer over him, an' on that man child ye shall think ivry day av your life. Think long, Dinah Shadd, for you'll niver have another tho' you pray till your knees are bleedin'. The mothers av children shall mock you behind your back whin you're wringin' over the wash-tub. You shall know what ut is to take a dhrunken husband home an' see him go to the gyard-room. Will that pl'ase you, Dinah Shadd,

14

that won't be seen talkin' to me daughter?
You shall talk to worse than Judy before
all's over. The sarjints' wives shall look
down on you, contemptuous daughter av a
sarjint, an' you shall cover ut all up wid a
smilin' face whin your heart's burstin'.
Stand off him, Dinah Shadd, for I've put the
black curse of Shielygh upon him, an' his
own mouth shall make ut good.'

"She pitched forward on her head an'
began foamin' at the mouth. Dinah Shadd
ran out wid water, and Judy dhragged the
ould woman into the veranda till she sat up.

"' I'm old an' forelore,' she sez, tremblin'
an' cryin', 'an' 'tis like I say a dale more
than I mane.'

"' When you're able to walk—go,' says
ould Mother Shadd. 'This house has no
place for the likes av you, that have cursed
me daughter.'

"' Eyah!' said the ould woman. 'Hard
words break no bones, an' Dinah Shadd 'll
kape the love av her husband till me bones
are green corn. Judy, darlin', I misremember what I came here for. Can you lend
us the bottom av a tay-cup av tay, Mrs.
Shadd?'

"But Judy dhragged her off, cryin' as tho'
her heart would break. An' Dinah Shadd
an' I, in ten minutes we had forgot ut all.''

"Then why do you remember it now?"
said I.

"Is ut like I'd forgit? Ivry word thaj

wicked ould woman spoke fell thrue in me
life aftherwards; an' I cud ha' stud ut all—
stud ut all, except fwhen little Shadd was
born. That was on the line av march
three months afther the rig'mint was taken
with cholera. We were betune Umballa an'
Kalka thin, an' I was on picket. When I
came off, the women showed me the child,
an' it turned on ut's side an' died as I looked.
We buried him by the road, an' Father Victor was a day's march behind wid the heavy
baggage, so the comp'ny captain read a
prayer. An' since then I've been a childless man, an' all else that ould Mother
Sheehy put upon me an' Dinah Shadd.
What do you think, sorr?"

I thought a good deal, but it seemed better then to reach out for Mulvaney's hand.
This demonstration nearly cost me the use
of three fingers. Whatever he knows of his
weaknesses, Mulvaney is entirely ignorant
of his strength.

"But what do you think?" he insisted, as
I was straightening out the crushed member.

My reply was drowned in yells and out-
cries from the next fire. where ten men were
shouting for " Orth'ris!" " Privit Orth'ris!"
" Mistah Or-ther-ris!" " Deah boy!" "Cap'n
Orth'ris!" "Field-Marshal Orth'ris!" "Stanley, you penn'orth o' pop, come 'ere to your
own comp'ny!" And the cockney, who had
been delighting another audience with re-
condite and Rabelaisian yarns, was shot

down among his admirers by the major force.

"You've crumpled my dress-shirt 'orrid," said he; "an' I sha'n't sing no more to this 'ere bloomin' drawin' room."

Learoyd, roused by the confusion, uncoiled himself, crept behind Ortheris, and raised him aloft on his shoulders.

"Sing, ye bloomin' hummin'-bird!" said he; and Ortheris, beating time on Learoyd's skull, delivered himself, in the raucous voice of the Ratcliffe Highway, of the following chaste and touching ditty:

> "My girl she give me the go oncet,
>   When I was a London lad,
> An' I went on the drink for a fortnight,
>   An' then I went to the bad.
> The queen she give me a shillin',
>   To fight for 'er over the seas;
> But guv'ment built me a fever-trap,
>   An' Injia give me disease.

*Chorus.*—"Ho! don't you 'eed what a girl says,
>   An' don't you go for the beer;
> But I was an ass when I was at grass,
>   An' that is why I'm 'ere.

> "I fired a shot at an Afghan;
>   The beggar 'e fired again;
> An' I lay on my bed with a 'ole in my 'ead,
>   An' missed the next campaign!
> I up with my gun at a Burman
>   Who carried a bloomin' *dah*,
> But the cartridge stuck an' the bay'nit bruk,
>   An' all I got was the scar.

*Chorus.*—" Ho ! don't you aim at a Afghan
　　　When you stand on the sky-line clear;
　　An' don't you go for a Burman
　　　If none o' your friends is near.

　　" I served my time for a corp'ral,
　　　An' wetted my stripes with pop,
　　For I went on the bend with a intimate
　　　friend,
　　　An' finished the night in the Shop.
　　I served my time for a sergeant ;
　　　The colonel 'e sez ' No !
　　The most you'll be is a full C. B.';*
　　　An'—very next night 'twas so.

*Chorus.*—" Ho ! don't you go for a corp'ral,
　　　Unless your 'ead is clear ;
　　But I was an ass when I was at grass,
　　　An' that is why I'm 'ere.

　　" I've tasted the luck o' the army
　　　In barrack an' camp an' clink,
　　An' I lost my tip through the bloomin'
　　　trip
　　　Along o' the women an' drink.
　　I'm down at the heel o' my service,
　　　An' when I am laid on the shelf,
　　My very wust friend from beginning to end,
　　　By the blood of a mouse, was myself.

*Chorus.*—" Ho ! don't you 'eed what a girl says,
　•　　An' don't you go for the beer ;
　　But I was an ass when I was at grass,
　　　An' that is why I'm 'ere."

" Ay, listen to our little man, now, singin'
an' shoutin' as tho' trouble had never touched

* Confined to barracks.

him! D'you remimber when he went mad
with homesickness?" said Mulvaney, recall-
ing a never-to-be-forgotten season when
Ortheris waded through the deep waters of
affliction and behaved abominably. "But
he's talkin' the bitter truth, tho'. Eyah!

> "Me very worst friend from beginning to end,
>     By the blood of a mouse, was mesilf.'

Harkout!" he continued, jumping to his
feet. "What did I tell you, sorr?"
    Fttl! spttl! whttl! went the rifles of the
picket in the darkness, and we heard their
feet rushing toward us as Ortheris tumbled
past me and into his great-coat. It is an
impressive thing, even in peace, to see an
armed camp spring to life with clatter of
accouterments, click of Martini levers, and
blood-curdling speculations as to the fate of
missing boots. "Pickets dhriven in," said
Mulvaney, staring like a buck at bay into the
soft, clinging gloom. "Stand by an' kape
close to us. If 'tis cav'lry, they may blun-
dher into the fires."
    *Tr—ra—ra!—ta—ra—la!* sung the thrice-
blessed bugle, and the rush to form square
began. There is much rest and peace in the
heart of a square if you arrive in time, and
are not trodden upon too frequently. The
smell of leather belts, fatigue uniform, and
packed humanity is comforting.
    A dull grumble, that seemed to come

from every point of the compass at once, struck our listening ears, and little thrills of excitement ran down the faces of the square. Those who write so learnedly about judging distance by sound should hear cavalry on the move at night. A high-pitched yell on the left told us that the disturbers were friends—the cavalry of the attack, who had missed their direction in the darkness, and were feeling blindly for some sort of support and camping-ground. The difficulty explained, they jingled on.

"Double pickets out there; by your arms lie down and sleep the rest," said the major, and the square melted away as the men scrambled for their places by the fires.

When I woke I saw Mulvaney, the night-dew gemming his mustache, leaning on his rifle at picket, lonely as Prometheus on his rock, with I know not what vultures tearing his liver.

# THE BIG DRUNK DRAF'.

We're goin' 'ome, we're goin' ome—
　　Our ship is *at* the shore,
An' you mus' pack your 'aversack,
　　For we won't come back no more.
Ho, don't you grieve for me,
　　My lovely Mary Ann,
For I'll marry you yet on a fourp'ny bit,
　　As a time-expired ma a an !
　　　　　　　　　*Barrack-room Ballad.*

An awful thing has happened! My
friend, Private Mulvaney, who went home
in the "Serapis," time-expired, not very
long ago, has come back to India as a civilian! It was all Dinah Shadd's fault. She
could not stand the poky little lodgings,
and she missed her servant Abdullah more
than words could tell. The fact was that
the Mulvaneys had been out here too long,
and had lost touch of England.

Mulvaney knew a contractor on one of
the new Central India lines, and wrote to
him for some sort of work. The contractor
said that if Mulvaney could pay the passage
he would give him command of a gang of
coolies for old sake's sake. The pay was
eighty-five rupees a month, and Dinah
Shadd said that if Terence did not accept

she would make his life a "blasted purgathory." Therefore the Mulvaneys came out
as "civilians," which was a great and terrible fall; though Mulvaney tried to disguise
it, by saying that he was "ker'nel on the
railway line, an' a consequinshal man."

He wrote me an invitation, on a tool-in-
dent form, to visit him; and I came down
to the funny little "construction" bungalow
at the side of the line. Dinah Shadd had
planted pease about and about, and nature
had spread all manner of green stuff round
the place. There was no change in Mulvaney except the change of raiment, which
was deplorable, but could not be helped.
He was standing upon his trolly, harang-
uing a gang-man, and his shoulders were as
well drilled, and his big, thick chin was as
clean-shaven as ever.

"I'm a civilian now," said Mulvaney.
"Cud you tell that I was iver a martial
man? Don't answer, sorr, av you're strain-
in' betune a complimint an' a lie. There's
no houldin' Dinah Shadd now she's got a
house av her own. Go inside an' dhrink tay
out av chiny in the drrrrawin'-room, an'
thin we'll drink like Christians undher the
tree here. Scut, ye naygur-folk! There's
a sahib come to call on me, an' that's more
than he'll iver do for you onless you run!
Get out, an' go on pilin' up the earth, quick,
till sundown."

When we three were comfortably settled

under the big *sisham* in front of the bungalow, and the first rush of questions and
answers about Privates Ortheris and Learoyd and old times and places had died
away, Mulvaney said, reflectively : "Glory
be there's no p'rade to-morrow, and no bun-
headed corp'ril-bhoy to give you his lip.
An' yit I don't know. 'Tis hard to be something ye niver were an' niver meant to be,
an' all the ould days shut up along wid
your papers. Eyah! I'm growin' rusty,
an' 'tis the will av God that a man mustn't
serve his quane for time an' all."

He helped himself to a fresh peg, and
sighed furiously.

"Let your beard grow, Mulvaney," said
I, "and then you won't be troubled with
those notions. You'll be a real civilian."

Dinah Shadd had confided to me in the
drawing-room her desire to coax Mulvaney
into letting his beard grow. "'Twas so
civilian-like," said poor Dinah, who hated
her husband's hankering for his old life.

"Dinah Shadd, you're a dishgrace to an
honust, clane-scraped man!" said Mulvaney,
without replying to me. "Grow a beard on
your own chin, darlint, and lave me razors
alone. They're all that stand betune me
and disris-pect-ability. Av I didn't shave,
I wud be torminted wid an outrajis thurrst;
for there's nothin' so dhryin' to the throat
as a big billy-goat waggin' undher the chin.
Ye wuldn't have me dhrink always, Dinah

Shadd? By the same token, you're kapin' me crool dhry. Let me look at that whisky."

The whisky was lent and returned, but Dinah Shadd, who had been just as eager as her husband in asking after old friends, rent me with:

"I take shame for you, sorr, comin' down here—though the saints know you're as welkim as the daylight whin you do come— an' upsettin' Terence's head wid your nonsense about—about fwhat's much better forgotten. He bein' a civilian now, an' you niver was aught else. Can you not let the army rest? 'Tis not good for Terence."

I took refuge by Mulvaney, for Dinah Shadd has a temper of her own.

"Let be—let be," said Mulvaney. " 'Tis only wanst in a way I can talk about the old days." Then to me: "Ye say Dhrumshticks is well, an' his lady tu? I niver knew how I liked the gray garron till I was shut av him an' Asia." ("Dhrumshticks" was the nickname of the colonel commanding Mulvaney's old regiment.) "Will ye be seein' him again? You will. Thin tell him"—Mulvaney's eyes began to twinkle —"tell him wid Privit"—

"Mister, Terence," interrupted Dinah Shadd.

"Now the divil an' all his angels an' the firmament av hiven fly away wid the 'Mister,' an' the sin av makin' me swear be on your own confession, Dinah Shadd! Privit,

I tell ye. Wid Privit Mulvaney's best obedience, that but for me the last time-expired
wud be still pullin' hair on their way to the
sea."

He threw himself back in the chair,
chuckled, and was silent.

"Mrs. Mulvaney," I said, "please take up
the whisky, and don't let him have it until
he has told the story."

Dinah Shadd dexterously whipped the
bottle away, saying at the same time, "'Tis
nothing to be proud av," and thus captured
by the enemy, Mulvaney spake:

"'Twas on Chuseday week. I was behad-
erin' round wid the gangs on the 'bankmint
—I've taught the hoppers how to kape step
an' stop screechin'—whin a head gang-man
comes up to me, wid about two inches av shirt-
tail hangin' round his neck an' a disthressful
light in his oi. 'Sahib,' sez he, 'there's a
rig'mint an' a half av soldiers up at the
junction, knockin' red cinders out av ivrything an' ivrybody! They thried to hang
me in me cloth,' he sez, 'an' there will be
murder an' ruin an' rape in the place before
nightfall! They say they're comin' down
here to wake us up. What will we do wid
our women-folk?'

"'Fetch me throlly!' sez I; 'me heart's
sick in me ribs for a wink at anything wid
the quane's uniform on ut. Fetch me
throlly, an' six of the jildiest men, an' run
me up in shtyle.'"

" He tuk his best coat," said Dinah Shadd reproachfully.

" 'Twas to do honor to the widdy. I cud ha' done no less, Dinah Shadd. You and your digreshins interfere wid the coorse av the narrative. Have you iver considhered fwhat I wud look like wid me head shaved as well as me chin? You bear that in mind, Dinah darlin'.

" I was throllied up six miles, all to get a squint at that draf'. I knew 'twas a spring draf' goin' home, for there's no rig'mint hereabouts, more's the pity."

" Praise the Virgin!" murmured Dinah Shadd. But Mulvaney did not hear.

" Whin I was about three quarters av a mile off the rest-camp, powtherin' along fit to burrst, I heard the noise av the men, an', on me sowl, sorr, I cud catch the voice av Peg Barney bellowin' like a bison wid the belly-ache. You remimber Peg Barney that was in D Comp'ny—a red, hairy scraun, wid a scar on his jaw? Peg Barney that cleared out the Blue Lights' Jubilee meeting wid the cook-room mop last year?

" Thin I knew ut was a draf' of the ould rig'mint, an' I was conshumed wid sorrow for the bhoy that was in charge. We was harrd scrapin's at any time. Did I iver tell you how Horker Kelley went into clink nakid as Phœbus Apollonius, wid the shirts av the corp'ril an' file undher his arrum? An' he was a moild man! But I'm digresh-

in'. 'Tis a shame both to the rig'mints an'
the arrmy sendin' down little orf'cer bhoys
wid a draf' av strong men mad wid liquor
an' the chanst av gettin' shut av India, an'
niver a punishment that's fit to be given
right down an' away from cantonmints to
the dock! 'Tis this nonsince. Whin I am
servin' me time, I'm undher the articles av
war, an' can be whipped on the peg for them.
But whin I served me time, I'm a Reserve
man, an' the articles av war haven't any
hould on me. An' orf'cer can't do anythin'
to a time-expired savin' confinin' him to
barricks. 'Tis a wise rig'lation, bekaze a
time-expired does not have any barricks,
bein' on the move all the time. 'Tis a Solo-
mon av a rig'lation, is that. I wud like to
be inthroduced to the man who secreted ut.
'Tis easier to get colts from a Kibbereen
horse-fair into Galway than to take a bad
draf' over tin miles av country. Consi-
quintly that rig'lation for fear that the men
wud be hurt by the little orf'cer boy. No
matther. The nearer me throlly came to
the rest-camp, the woilder was the shine,
an' the louder was the voice av Peg Barney.
'' 'Tis good I am here,' thinks I to meself,
'for Peg alone is employmint to two or
three.' He bein', I well knew, as copped as
a dhrover.

"Faith, that rest-camp was a sight! The
tent-ropes was all skew-nosed, an' the pegs
looked as dhrunk as the mer.—fifty av thim

—the scourin's an' rinsin's an' divil's lavin's av the ould rig'mint. I tell you, sorr, they were dhrunker than any men you've ever seen in your mortial life. How does a draf' get dhrunk? How does a frog get fat? They suk ut in through their shkins.

"There was Peg Barney sittin' on the groun' in his shirt—wan shoe off an' wan shoe on—whackin' a tent-peg over the head wid his boot, an' singin' fit to wake the dead. 'Twas no clane song that he sung, though. 'Twas the 'Divil's Mass.'"

"What's that?" I asked.

"Whin a bad egg is shut av the arrmy, he sings the 'Divil's Mass' for a good riddance; an' that means swearin' at ivrything from the commandher-in-chief down to the room-corp'ril, such as you niver in your days heard. Some men can swear to make green turf crack! Have you iver heard the curse in an Orange lodge? The 'Divil's Mass' is tin times worse, an' Peg Barney was singin' ut, whackin' the tent-peg on the head wid his boot for each man that he cursed. A powerful big voice had Peg Barney, an' a hard swearer he was whin sober. I stood forninst him, an' 'twas not me oi alone that cud tell Peg was dhrunk as a coot.

"'Good-mornin', Peg,' sez I, whin he dhrew breath afther cursin' the adj'tint-gin'ral; 'I've put on me best coat to see you, Peg Barney,' sez I.

"'Thin take ut off again,' sez Peg Barney,

latherin' away wid the boot; 'take ut off an' dance, ye lousy civilian!'

"Wid that he begins cursin' ould Dhrumshticks, being so full he clean misremimbers the brigade-major an' the judge advokit gin'ral.

"'Do you not know me, Peg?' sez I, though me blood was hot in me wid being called a civilian."

"An' him a decent married man!" wailed Dinah Shadd.

"'I do not,' sez Peg, 'but dhrunk or sober I'll tear the hide off your back wid a shovel whin I've stopped singin'.'

"'Say you so, Peg Barney?' sez I. ''Tis clear as mud you've forgotten me. I'll assist your autobiography.' Wid that I stretched Peg Barney, boot an' all, an' wint into the camp. An awful sight ut was!

"'Where's the orf'cer in charge av the detachment?' sez I to Scrub Greene—the manest little worm that ever walked.

"'There's no orf'cer, ye ould cook,' sez Scrub; 'we're a bloomin' republic.'

"'Are you that?' sez I; 'thin I'm O'Connell the Dictator, an' by this you will larn to kape a civil tongue in your rag-box.'

"Wid that I stretched Scrub Greene an' wint to the orf'cer's tent. 'Twas a new little bhoy—not wan I'd iver seen before. He was sittin' in his tent, purtendin' not to 'ave ear av the racket.

"I saluted—but for the life av me I mint

to shake hands whin I wint in. 'Twas the
sword hangin' on the tent-pole changed me
will.

"'Can't I help, sorr?' sez I; ''tis a strong
man's job they've given you, an' you'll be
wantin' help by sundown.' He was a bhoy
wid bowils, that child, an' a rale gintleman.

"'Sit down,' sez he.

"'Not before me orf'cer,' sez I; an' I
tould him fwhat me service was.

"'I've heard av you,' sez he. 'You tuk
the town of Lungtungpen nakid.'

"'Faith,' thinks I, 'that's honor an'
glory;' for 'twas Lift'nint Brazenose did that
job. 'I'm wid ye, sorr,' sez I, 'if I'm av
use. They shud niver ha' sent you down
wid the draf'. Savin' your prisince, sorr,' I
sez, ''tis only Lift'nint Hackerston in the
ould rig'mint can manage a home draf'.'

"'I've never had charge of men like this
before,' sez he, playin' wid the pens on the
table; 'an' I see by the rig'lations—'

"'Shut your oi to the rig'lations, sorr,' I
sez, ' till the throoper's into blue wather. By
the rig'lations you've got to tuck thim up
for the night, or they'll be runnin' foul av
me coolies an' makin' a shiverarium half
through the country. Can you trust your
non-coms, sorr?'

"'Yes,' sez he.

"'Good,' sez I; 'there'll be throuble before the night. Are you marchin', sorr?'"

"'To the next station,' sez he.

15

"'Better still,' sez I ; 'there'll be big throuble.'

"'Can't be too hard on a home draf',' sez he ; 'the great thing is to get thim in-ship.'

"'Faith, you've larnt the half av your lesson, sorr,' sez I, 'but av you shtick to the rig'lations you'll niver get thim in-ship at all, at all. Or there won't be a rag av kit betune thim whin you do.'

"'Twas a dear little orf'cer bhoy, an' by way av kapin' his heart up, I tould him fwhat I saw wanst in a draf' in Egypt."

"What was that, Mulvaney?" said I.

"Sivin-an'-fifty men sittin' on the bank av a canal, laughin' at a poor little squidgereen av an orf'cer that they'd made wade into the slush an' pitch the things out av the boats for their lord high mightinesses. That made the orf'cer boy woild wid indignation.

"'Soft an' aisy, sorr,' sez I ; 'you've niver had your draf' in hand since you left cantonmints. Wait till the night, an' your work will be ready to you. Wid your permission, sorr, I will investigate the camp, an' talk to me ould frins. 'Tis no manner av use thryin' to shtop the divilmint now.'

"Wid that I wint out into the camp an' inthrojuced mesilf to ivry man sober enough to remimber me. I was some wan in the ould days, an' the bhoys was glad to see me —all excipt Peg Barney, wid a eye like a tomato five days in the bazaar, an' a nose

to correspon'. They come round me an'
shuk me, an' I tould thim I was in privit
employ wid an income av me own, an' a
drrrawin'-room fit to bate the quane's; an'
wid me lies an' me shtories an' nonsince
gin'rally I kept 'em quiet in wan way an'
another, knockin' roun' the camp. 'Twas
bad even thin whin I was the Angel av
Peace.

" I talked to me ould non-coms—they was
sober—an' betune me an' thim we wore the
draf' over into their tents at the proper
time. The little orf'cer bhoy he comes
round, decint and civil-spoken as might
be.

" ' Rough quarters, men,' sez he, ' but
you can't look to be as comfortable as in
barricks. We must make the best av things.
I've shut me eyes to a dale av dog's trick
to-day, an' now there must be no more av
ut.'

" ' No more we will. Come an' have a
dhrink, me son,' sez Peg Barney, staggerin'
where he stud. Me little orf'cer bhoy kep
his timper.

" ' You're a sulky swine, ye are,' sez Peg
Barney, an' at that the men in the tent began
to laugh.

" I tould ye me orf'cer bhoy had bowils.
He cut Peg Barney as near as might be on
the oi that I'd squashed whin we first met.
Peg wint spinnin' acrost the tent.

" ' Peg him out, sorr,' sez I, in a whishper.

" ' Peg him out !' sez me orf'cer bhoy, up loud, just as if 'twas battalion p'rade, an' he pickin' his wurruds from the sarjint.

" The non-coms tuk Peg Barney—a howlin' handful he was—an' in three minuts he was pegged out—chin down, tight-drawn— on his stummick, a peg to each arm an' leg, swearin' fit to turn a naygur white.

" I tuk a peg an' jammed ut into his ugly jaw. 'Bite on that, Peg Barney,' I sez : 'the night is settin' frosty, an' you'll be wantin' divarsion before the mornin'. But for the rig'lations you'd be bitin' on a bullet now at the thriangles, Peg Barney,' sez I.

" All the draf' was out av their tents watchin' Barney bein' pegged.

" ' 'Tis ag'in the rig'lations ! He strook him !' screeches out Scrub Greene, who was always a lawyer ; an' some av the men tuk up the shoutin'.

" ' Peg out that man !' sez me orf'cer bhoy, niver losin' his timper; an' the non-coms went in an' pegged out Scrub Greene by the side av Peg Barney.

" I could see that the draf' was comin' roun'. The men stud, not knowin' fwhat to do.

" ' Get to your tents !' sez me orf'cer bhoy. 'Sarjint, put a sintry over these two men.'

" The men wint back into the tents like jackals, an' the rest av the night there was no noise at all excipt the stip av the sintry over the two, an' Scrub Greene blubberin'

like a child.   'Twas a chilly night, an' faith
ut sobered Peg Barney.

"Just before revelly, me orf'cer bhoy
comes out an' sez: 'Loose those men an'
sind thim to their tents!'   Scrub Greene
wint away widout a word, but Peg Barney
stiff wid the cowld, stud like a sheep, thryin'
to make his orf'cer understhand he was
sorry for playin' the goat.

"There was no tucker in the draf' whin
ut fell in for the march, an' divil a wurrd
about 'illegality' could I hear.

"I wint to the ould color-sarjint an' I
sez, 'Let me die in glory,' sez I.   'I've
seen a man this day!'

"'A man he is,' sez ould Hother; 'the
draf's as sick as a herrin.'   They'll all go
down to the sea like lambs.   That bhoy has
the bowils av a cantonmint av gin'rals.'

"'Amin,' sez I, 'an' good luck go wid
him, wheriver he be, by land or by sea.
Let me know how the draf' gets clear.'

"An' do you know how they did?   That
bhoy, so I was tould by letters from Bombay, bullydamned 'em down to the dock,
till they cudn't call their sowls their own.
From the time they left me oi till they was
'tween decks, not wan av thim was more
than dacintly dhrunk.   An', by the holy
articles av war, whin they wint aboard they
cheered him till they cudn't spake, an' that,
mark you, has not come about wid a draf' in
the mim'ry av livin' man!   You look to

that little orf'cer bhoy. He has bowils. 'Tis not ivry child that wud chuck the rig'lations to Flanders an' stretch Peg Barney on a wink from a broken an' dilapidated ould carkiss like mesilf. I'd be proud to serve—"

"Terence, you're a civilian," said Dinah Shadd, warningly.

"So I am—so I am. Is ut likely I wud forget ut? But he was a gran' bhoy, all the same, an' I'm only a mudtipper wid a hod on me shoulthers. The whisky's in the heel av your hand, sorr. Wid your good lave we'll dhrink to the ould rig'mint—three fingers—standin' up!"

And we drank.